OVER THE TOP

MONTANA MAVERICKS
BOOK FOUR

REBECCA ZANETTI

This one's for Anissa Beatty - thank you for all that you do!

A SPECIAL THANK YOU

I want to extend my heartfelt thanks to Cathie Bailey from the Quapaw Tribe for her invaluable insights and thoughtful feedback on my story. Your perspective and generosity in sharing your knowledge enriched the narrative in ways I couldn't have achieved on my own. I'm deeply grateful for the time, care, and expertise you brought to this project, helping ensure the story resonates with authenticity and respect. Thank you for being part of this journey.

CHAPTER 1

Make a man feel special, and he'll follow you like a chestnut wanting a carrot. ~ The Lady Elks Secret Archives.

HAWK RAIN SAT BACK in the chair at the round table, his gaze on the frothy mug of Wallace Pale Ale in front of him. As usual for a Saturday night, Adam's bar in downtown Mineral Lake was hopping with ranchers kicking back with microbrews, peanuts, and loud laughs. Cheerful Christmas decorations covered every wall, and colorful lights sparkled from behind the bar.

The place smelled like pine, beer, and home, but the cozy atmosphere failed to calm him. Apparently the bar had purchased new glasses. The thought irritated him, and he couldn't figure out why.

"What are you moping about?" The question came from Colton Freeze, his best friend, and held no judgment. Just thoughtful contemplation.

"Nothin'." Hawk took another drink, eyeing Colt, who sprawled in his chair after a long day of punching cows.

The guy's hair almost reached his shoulders in a myriad of

cool colors—black, reddish blond and brown—from his Native American and Irish ancestry that somehow blended together. His blue eyes were dark and serious, his jawline scruffy, and his shoulders stiff. "Huh. *Nothin'.* Are you all right?" Colt asked.

If one more person in town asked Hawk how he was doing or if he was okay, he was going to pummel them. "Adam bought new mugs."

Colton shoved a cowboy hat back on his head. "So?"

So? Hawk had been gone too long, taking care of business, and things had changed. So had he, but nobody could see the damage that had been done to his psyche. "I liked the old mugs." He lifted his, which was heavier than the former ones.

Colton's chair scraped on the scarred wooden floor as he pushed back from the table, his lip twisting. "We're talking about mugs instead of anything serious now?"

"Yes." If Hawk's buddy wanted to get deep and talk about feelings, he could go chat with his very knocked-up wife.

"Fine. Are you home for good this time?" Colton asked.

Hawk sighed. "No."

"Well, that displeases me, because I figured you were in Mineral Lake for good last time, then I got married, and then you disappeared," Colt murmured.

"I had something to take care of—and I can't talk about it." Hawk had signed on for a civilian mission, and he didn't regret one second. Especially since he'd actually lived through it and made it home. "The job isn't finished, not really, and I'm just here to rest up." The idea that he'd be able to finish the job, to completely destroy Meyer's organization, was too much to hope for.

"I'm tired of the secrecy, and I'm ready to help." Colton tapped his fingers on the table. "I know you're still working for Reese."

"Yep." Hawk took another drink. Reese was a former DEA agent turned private security guru, who had hired Hawk right out of the military for one big job. One that wasn't over yet. "Reese is a good guy."

"I know." Colton turned as a light swept across the stage at the far end of the room, and a cheer went through the boisterous crowd. His mouth tightened. "She is *not* wearing enough clothes."

Hawk's entire body went on full alert as he took in the lead singer—his friend's little sister. Dawn Freeze sidled up to the mic dressed in a tiny skirt that barely covered her ass and revealed long and lean legs encased in cowboy boots. Red and black cowboy boots.

His balls pulled tight and bellowed a hello.

The stunning minx wore one of those fancy bustiers that pushed up what had to be perfect breasts. A saucy black cowboy hat perched on her head, and even across the room, Hawk could see the amused sparkle in her dangerous eyes.

Blue didn't come close to describing those eyes, and he'd go to the grave before admitting it, but they were the last image that had flashed through his brain before he'd nearly died the year before.

He may have even whispered her name before falling unconscious.

That was in the past, and any thought of claiming her would stay there as well. He was about as screwed up as a guy could be, and he was smart enough to know it. Plus, there'd come a time when he wouldn't make it home from a job, and he couldn't leave his girl behind like that. Especially a sweetheart like Dawn. When she gave her loyalty, it was forever, because the woman was all or nothing and always had been.

He shifted in his seat to ease the pain of his suddenly raging cock and took a deep drink of the potent brew. This was no big deal, and he was out for fun with his best friend.

Then Dawn opened her mouth and started to sing.

A groan rumbled from his chest. Sexy and surprisingly

husky, Dawn's voice wrapped around the room, focused hard, and licked right up his dick.

He downed half his beer, and the cold drink slammed into his gut.

Colton grinned and slapped him on the back. "The girl can sing, though. Right?"

Clueless. Fucking clueless. Hawk managed a smile and a nod.

Colton continued, "We didn't like her singing in a bar, but what the heck. It's not like we haven't taught her how to maim anybody who bothers her."

Hawk had taught her to go for the eyes, back in kindergarten when Billy Nolan had pulled her hair. "I figured she'd quit singing now that she's working for the family company."

Colt shrugged. "She likes to sing, too."

Yeah. With a voice like that, she could probably go far if she had any interest in being famous. Which she didn't. "What's up with all the pink?" The decorations were pink, the band wore pink...even the drum set was pink.

"It's Sizzled Pink. They're a traveling band, and Dawn sang for them a few times during college." Colton shook his head. "Sometimes I think she's a little tempted to keep singing, but then I figure she'd rather stay home and get settled in her new job as VP of Finances for Lodge-Freeze Enterprises."

Hawk nodded. While Dawn liked to sing, it had never truly been her passion. He knew her, understood her wants. At one point, *he'd* been what she'd wanted.

Maybe he still was.

But she was one of a kind, and she deserved the whole package, with a guy who wasn't half-crazed sometimes by the feeling of an imaginary riflescope catching his every move. He was safe now, but he couldn't get rid of the expectation of imminent attack...yet. At some point, he'd feel peace again, and he was working hard on it. He'd spent the last eight months taking care of the biggest threat hanging over his head, which he hadn't thought he'd be able to do. If he could take down the rest of the organization, and live through it, then...maybe?

But dating Dawn would seriously strain his relationship with Colton and Colt's older brothers, and Hawk needed them. They were family. However, Dawn Freeze was special, and a chance with her might be worth the risk. As usual, when he thought of her, his thoughts zinged around his brain until his ears rang.

Her gaze met his, and her voice lowered to a huskier tone. Those eyes softened, and she stepped closer to the mic, her hands wrapping around the base.

Nothing was too much to give to have those hands on him. He lacked the strength to look away. Or maybe it was the will to look away. So he watched her, allowing her to dig deep into his soul as the music rose in tempo.

The song finally ended, and he exhaled, not realizing he'd been holding his breath.

A shadow crossed between their table and the bar lights as steps clipped closer. Colton smiled, his tough expression mellowing. "Melanie." Standing, he yanked back a chair for his more than eight-months pregnant wife, who was dusting snow off her puffy jacket.

Hawk half stood and waited until Mel sat. Then he stiffened as Colt pulled out another chair for Anne Newberry, Colt's secretary. The curvy blonde dropped into the chair with a sigh of relief, her thick boots scattering slush. He hadn't realized the women would be joining them.

Melanie reached to tug him into a side-hug. "I'm so glad you're home."

Emotion pricked the back of his eyes, and he gingerly returned the embrace. "Me, too." He'd been best friends with Mel and Colt since early childhood, and he'd missed her. When she and Colton had finally gotten together, the relief Hawk had felt at knowing they'd both be safe and protected had floored him. The pregnancy had added a translucent glow to her smooth skin, or maybe that was just the love obviously there for her husband as she winked at Colton.

"I hope you don't mind that Anne and I joined you guys." Melanie pulled a bowl of peanuts her way to grab a handful. "We went shopping and figured it'd be fun to watch Dawn sing."

Hawk forced yet another smile. "That's great." Now Dawn would think he was on a double date, and the last thing he wanted to do was hurt her. Sure, he couldn't make a move on her right now. But shoving another woman in her face was something he'd never do. Her crush on him wasn't exactly a town secret.

In Mineral Lake, Montana, located dead center in Maverick County...town secrets didn't exist.

Colton ordered lemonade for Melanie and a beer for Anne from a waitress they'd all known since grade school. The music continued while Hawk tried to engage in conversation and appear normal.

Was Dawn watching? He tried to capture her gaze several times, but she kept busy entertaining the crowd. She really could sing.

The night droned on, and finally he figured he'd just stay late and explain to Dawn that this wasn't a double date—in case she cared. Maybe she wouldn't mind. Or maybe he'd hurt her feelings by drinking with another woman under her nose—date or not. Either way, he needed to explain.

Yeah, he was pathetic.

The music wound down, and his body finally started to mellow as the band stopped playing.

Melanie gasped next to him.

Adrenaline swamped his system. "Mel?" he asked, reaching for his keys.

Her brown eyes widened, and delight lifted her lips. Grabbing his hand, she pressed his palm to her abdomen. "Feel."

Womp. Womp, womp, womp. A little foot drummed against his hand. Heat roared through him, and for the first time, a genuine smile tickled his lips. His shoulders relaxed. "The kid can kick."

"Kids." Melanie grinned and patted Hawk's knuckles.

Hawk leaned back. "Kids? As in you have more than one in there?" He glanced down at Mel's protruding tummy, and his smile spread.

She chuckled. "Yep. Two. Probably girls."

"Boys," Colton said.

Hawk would never understand why they didn't just find out the sex of the babies, but he figured a kick like that was probably from a girl. A rambunctious, feisty, sweet girl like her mama...and now there were two mini-Mel's on the way. God help the town.

"I can't wait to see the little ones." His chest lightened in a way it hadn't in over a year. Two babies coming. Hope for the future, and for once, he could actually feel it. He laughed out loud.

Anne pushed back from the table. "Speaking of little ones, I have to get home to Tyler."

Hawk and Colton instantly stood. The single mom was often busy, and her husband had died in a construction accident. With no family, Anne had headed west to start a new life for her and her kid. Of course, the Lodge-Freeze clan had instantly folded them into the family.

Colton whistled at Adam behind the bar. "Just put it on my tab."

Adam nodded, while his attention remained on the band as they packed up.

Hawk rubbed his chin. Adam had purchased the bar after attending business school, which he'd done after a stint in the military. They'd bonded right away and had been friends for years. In fact, Adam had sent more than one care package to Hawk overseas. "Why isn't Adam playing the guitar?" Hawk asked.

Colton grinned. "Bar fight last week. Adam had to step in and sprained his wrist. Looks like he took off the bandage, though."

"How's the bar doing?" Hawk asked.

Colton helped Melanie from her chair, biting his lip as she groaned and lifted her big belly. "Seems to be doing good. We're supportive."

Mel snorted. "We do our best." She leaned up on her toes to brush a kiss across Hawk's jaw. "Come for dinner tomorrow night."

The gentle touch felt like home. "Yes, ma'am," he said. His mama, God rest her soul, had taught him not to refuse a woman offering a guy home-cooked food. Plus, Melanie was one of the best cooks in Maverick County. "I'll be there."

Colton lifted an eyebrow. "You leaving right now?"

"I'll be along shortly." Hawk pointed to his half-full glass.

"Okay." Colton herded the women through the nearly empty bar. Once the band stopped playing, folks usually headed home. The band began packing up amid calls of "good night" and "see ya next Friday".

Hawk sat and finished his beer, his gut churning. He hadn't seen Dawn in months, although he'd answered every letter or email she'd sent. They'd kept the conversation simple and had focused on home.

Two of the waitresses cashed out and stomped out into the wintery night. Then a couple of the band members. Adam disappeared into the back room.

Hawk stood and shifted his weight. He took off his cowboy hat to set on the table. He cleared his throat. Maybe he should sit back down.

Dawn swept around the drum set and headed his way. Her smile was one of the prettiest things he'd ever seen.

Without an ounce of hesitation, she barreled right into his arms.

Warmth and woman. His arms tightened around her, but he kept his hold light. She had such a large personality, he forgot how small she was. The woman didn't even reach his chin.

Her scent of wild huckleberries wafted around him, slammed into his heart, and zinged down to his groin.

He swallowed and stepped back, his throat threatening to close. "You were amazing tonight."

Delight danced across her face. She lifted her head to meet his eyes, hers like blue diamonds sparkling against classic features. Her mother was Native American, her father a spirited Irishman, and she'd inherited the best from both—beautiful blue eyes and long, silky black hair. "Thanks. I'm so glad you're home."

He cleared his throat. Then he grabbed his hat off the table to twist in his hands. "I, ah, wanted to explain."

Her gaze stayed so warm it nearly thawed him. The woman was glad to see him, and damned if that didn't feel good. A tiny wrinkle creased between her arched brows. "Huh?"

The last thing he wanted to do was hurt her, but they had to get things straight now. The old crush she had on him needed to be buried. "I wasn't on a date with Anne."

Dawn stretched her back, pushing out those glorious breasts. "Okay."

He shook his head, trying to concentrate on the moment and not her amazing tits. Colton would rightfully kick his ass for going there. "I just didn't want you to think I'd come in here on a date."

Dawn stilled. She blinked and then narrowed her focus to his face. "Why not?"

Because the woman had crushed on him big time, and that didn't just go away. "I don't want to hurt you."

Her smile held a hint of danger. "Do I look hurt?"

Hell no. She looked like an angel fully prepared to sin. "You know what I mean."

She bit her lip, and he wanted to groan. Again. "I really don't know, Hawk. Last time I checked, we were just friends. You made that abundantly clear last year."

Yeah, he had. He'd said those exact words to her after Colt and Melanie's wedding, figuring there wasn't a chance he'd survive his last job and make it home. Yet here he was. "I just wanted to make sure we were on the same page." He sounded like a jerk.

Then she smiled, and he forgot to breathe. Again. "We're on the same page," she murmured.

The end of the bar slammed open, and Adam strode around with a thick blue ski jacket in his hands. "Hawk. It's good to see you."

Hawk leaned over for a half-hug. "Ditto. We'll have a drink sometime this week."

"Name the night, and I'm here." Adam turned toward Dawn. "Sorry I took so long."

Hawk frowned and eyed the bar owner. The guy was well over six foot, built tough, and smiling way too gently. "Took so long?"

Dawn chuckled. "Were you counting your money from tonight? Miser?"

Adam grinned, flashing what people probably thought was a charming dimple. "I've asked you repeatedly to stop calling me that." He helped Dawn into the thick jacket. "You ready?" His smile relaxed his usually hard face.

Dawn patted Adam's flat stomach and turned back to Hawk. "I think so. Are we done?"

Hawk slowly nodded. "Yeah." Almost in a daze, he followed

Adam and Dawn from the bar, waiting until Adam locked up. How could they be dating? Did Colton know about that? How could this have happened so quickly? "You two have a nice night."

"Thanks." Dawn smiled, and the duo ran through the sleet and across the street to a silver Chevy pickup against the opposite curb. Adam opened the driver's door, and Dawn jumped up, scooting across the seat. Two seconds later, Adam started the engine and drove the truck down the deserted main street of town, festive Christmas lights lighting the way.

Hawk watched them until the truck disappeared. Snow and freezing rain smashed down, and he didn't care. Heat exploded in his chest, forcing him to take several deep breaths to calm himself.

All he'd wanted to do was explain to Dawn that he respected her and would never hurt her feelings as a friend. The last thing he expected was to find himself figuratively standing in the snow with his dick in his hand.

CHAPTER 2

Give a man some competition, because boys like to fight. ~ The Lady Elks Secret Archives

DAWN FINISHED SETTING out the bingo cards, her mind spinning. The second floor of the Elks Lodge held a wide bar, a hodge-podge of tables, and real leather chairs that were now back in style. The floor, walls, and high ceiling were all built about a hundred years ago with wood from the local forest. Dancing Santas lined one wall, while stacks of colorful poinsettias were placed all around the room.

What in the world had happened last night? First Hawk showed up looking all wounded and sexy. Then he'd partied with Colton and had seemed more detached than ever, not even lighting up when Melanie had arrived. Finally, the guy had apologized for hanging out with friends.

The only time, definitely the *only time*, the man had seemed present was when their eyes had connected during the first set. She'd felt that connection down to her toes—and everywhere in between.

She bit back a grin upon remembering the look on his face when she'd left with Adam, who'd just been helping her out while her car was in the shop. Yeah. Call her petty, call her immature, but that had felt great.

Dumb-ass men.

"Are you ready, dear?" Mrs. Hudson asked, shoving wire rimmed glasses up her tiny nose as she bustled across the wide room. The spitfire was almost five feet tall with curly white hair, a perfectly symmetrical nose, and powdery skin. She'd been widowed sometime around the early sixties, had reportedly been quite wild for a while, and for the last year or so, had seemed content dating her wrinkled neighbor with no commitment.

Tonight she'd worn a lime-green tracksuit with "Juicy" bejeweled down one short leg. Someone had given the ancient gossip a BeJewler the previous Christmas, and everything she wore sparkled. *Really* sparkled.

"Yes, ma'am." Dawn gestured toward the pretty red tablecloths adorning the scarred wooden tables. "Just have a seat, and as soon as everyone arrives, we'll start calling those numbers." She glanced around. "After tonight, we need to start decorating for the winter dance."

"Yes. Thanks again for planning the dance this year. It'll be a doozy." Mrs. Hudson snapped her fingers toward her beau, Henry Bullton, who had just finished pouring a series of Cosmos into Martini glasses. "Henry? This is girl time," she chirped.

The retired car salesman scratched his thinning gray hair and lumbered around the bar. His khaki pants dragged on the floor, and he hitched them up almost to his armpits. "All right. I'll pick ya up after bingo." He bowed, and cherry cough drops plunked from his pocket. "Darn." Leaning over, he grimaced and then reloaded the pockets. "We'll go to my place." He grinned and sauntered out the door.

"We most certainly will not," Mrs. Hudson called loudly before turning back toward Dawn. "Men." She reached into a glittering bag nearly large enough to span from her shoulder to her knees. "I made you something." She grunted and tugged out a hand-stitched pillow. Then she turned and glanced at a group of ladies setting up the coffee table near the wide wall of windows facing Mineral Lake. "Girls? Now, please." The *please* was for etiquette...because there was a clear order barked into the words.

Three white-haired heads bobbed, and then Maverick County's elite Board of Lady Elks bustled their way.

Dawn swallowed, her instincts humming.

Mrs. Hudson waited until the seniors properly surrounded Dawn before flourishing the pillow. "We had a vote at our last meeting, which was at Mertyl's house, because we had to do something while she ordered out. Burned the rolls, you know."

Mertyl Franks, the mayor's mother, gasped. "Now you hush your mouth, Patty Hudson. You know my oven has been on the blink."

Mrs. Hudson waved her hand. "Please stay on task, girls. Anyway, we voted to help you find a man. It's time, Dawn Freeze."

Oh no. *No, no, no, no, no.* Dawn tried to back away, only to be surrounded by shriveled people. Most folks would think the meddling cute, but Dawn had grown up in Maverick County. The women were serious, and they'd hound her. Really, really hound her. She waved her hands, trying to keep the panic at bay. "That's so kind of you, Mrs. Hudson. But as you know, I just started a new job—"

"Job, schmob," Georgiana Millbury—of Millbury Grocery— scoffed, flipping her long hair. "A job won't make your mama a grandma, or keep your bed warm at night."

Okay. Dawn could handle this, and it truly needed to be handled quickly before things got out of control. "My mother is already a grandma from Jake, and she's about to be a grandma from Colton. Besides, I have plenty of blankets on my bed."

Mrs. Bernie Poppins, ex-librarian, narrowed faded eyes. "If you think blankets warm a bed, we need to have a different discussion later tonight. For now, you need to understand, we care very much about choosing the right man."

"I voted for Adam," Mrs. Millbury said, her chin wobbling. She had several inches in height on Mrs. Hudson and kept her posture ramrod straight to take advantage of being able to see over everyone's heads.

"Not Adam." Mrs. Hudson glared at Mrs. Millbury. "That boy isn't ready to settle down, and if you ask me, there's a woman already tunneling into his heart." She turned back to Dawn. "Unless you're sweet on Adam. Then we could probably make him fall for you."

"No." Dawn shook her head. Did Adam have a love somewhere? He did seem kind of lonely sometimes, and she enjoyed his friendship, which didn't include her three older brothers—something rare in the town. "Adam and I are just buddies."

"Told you." Mrs. Hudson said. "After we discussed each candidate, it was so obvious that we really didn't debate long. Surely you know who we chose."

Dawn tried to head off the suggestion. "Hawk isn't ready—"

All four ladies sighed and nodded vigorously.

Mrs. Hudson slapped the pillow against Dawn's chest. "Yep. You called it. You've mooned over that boy for decades, and he's been alone for too long. Heck. He's practically part of your family already."

Mrs. Millbury clapped her hands together. "You knew it was Hawk, so it must be fate."

Of course it was Hawk. She had dreamed silly fantasies about the guy since she'd become old enough to notice the difference between boys and girls. "Hawk doesn't like me that way." Yeah, the truth hurt, but it was all she had to stop this train wreck.

So when all four ladies threw back their heads and laughed, she could only gape.

Mrs. Hudson wiped her eyes. "He doesn't like you. Youth is so wasted on you young'uns. Of course he likes you. If not, we're gonna help you *make* him like you."

Heat climbed into Dawn's face. Panic flirted with embarrassment, and she scrambled for a way out. "I can land my own dates, ladies."

Mrs. Hudson shook her head. "Forget dates. You need love and happily ever after. Obviously you're not making that happen on your own."

Dawn tried to sidle away from the huddle. Footsteps echoed on the stairs outside the room, and several more Lady Elks walked inside, stomping snow off their boots first. Her friend, Luann, followed the pack, saw the cluster of women around Dawn, and then made a sharp left for the bar. Traitor.

"Read the pillow," Mrs. Hudson said. "We Lady Elks have rules passed down for generations."

Oh man, this wasn't going to be good. Her hands shaking, Dawn turned over the pillow to read the list of five rules perfectly embroidered across it.

This couldn't possibly be happening.

How to Catch a Man
1. Make your man the only man around.
2. Don't give the cow away (AKA NO SEX).
3. The way to his heart really is through his stomach.
4. Let your man rescue you.
5. Give him the illusion of control so you can chase him until he catches you.

. . .

EACH LINE HAD BEEN CAREFULLY hand-stitched into perfect, even formation. Dawn breathed out, her shoulders relaxing as she clutched at a definite lifeline. "Darn it. I already broke number one last night by leaving Hawk at the bar and heading out with Adam last night. Shoot." She attempted to return the pillow to Mrs. Hudson.

Wrinkles plummeted together into a frown on Mrs. Poppins's face. "How did Hawk look when you left with Adam?"

Dawn paused. Surprised, irritated, and...lost. Hawk had looked lost standing alone in the snow, and at the thought, her heart thumped. Hard. "He looked just fine and happy to be heading home."

"Hmmm." Mrs. Hudson glanced around at her posse. "That's all right. Really, number one doesn't count much. So long as you follow the rest of the list, you'll get your man."

"Hawk isn't my man." The words hurt, even though she'd spent the last lonely months accustoming herself to that fact... and the reality that he'd never be hers. She liked him, and she wanted him in her life—even as a friend. So she'd had to let go. "Hawk will never be mine."

Mrs. Hudson's chin firmed. "Oh, sister. He will be. I promise."

Dawn shook off the odd feeling of Mrs. Hudson calling her *sister* and hustled over to the bar, where Luann drank a Wallace Brewery Huckleberry Ale. Luann was the lead guitarist for Sizzled Pink, and at school they'd often played bars together. When she'd said she needed to talk, Dawn had asked her up to the Elks for a drink. "Sorry. Now what did you want to chat about?" Dawn asked. "I have a couple of minutes before bingo starts."

Luann pushed streaked purple hair over her shoulder, her green eyes sparkling. "Nice pillow."

"Be quiet." Dawn bit back a chuckle, stuffing the cushion onto the barstool beside her. "They mean well, but seriously, they won't let up. Together, strong and banded, they're dangerous. Trust me."

Luann, who was originally from Houston, just chuckled. The two had become friends in college, sharing fun nights singing, but Dawn had studied finance, and Luann Eastern Philosophy. Then they'd traveled to Berlin for a couple of post-college intensives that lasted six months, and they'd had an amazing time. "Whatever. Are you ready to ditch the small town and come on tour with us? We booked a place in Paris and are going to take Europe by storm this time. Please come."

Dawn grinned. "While touring Europe with Sizzled Pink would be a blast, I just started at the family company and need to work on updating the software and double-checking the current investments." She'd traveled enough and wanted to be home. She glanced over her shoulder to where Mrs. Hudson was carefully picking through bingo cards for just the right one. "I like it here, and I'm ready to hang tight for a while."

Luann rolled her eyes. "You're ready to hang tight with Hawk Rain for a while, and I get that. He's a serious Hottie McHottie of Hottieness." She leaned forward, losing her smile. "He also has one combat boot out the door, if you ask me. Even while watching you sing last night, he didn't relax. Not once."

Dawn swallowed. Hawk never stayed home for long, and there wasn't any sign that he'd changed. Sure, she'd thought that once she'd finally graduated with her many degrees, he'd see her as all grown up. Maybe he had finally understood she was an adult, but that hadn't stopped him from leaving. While he was home now, he might not stay. "Even if Hawk takes off again, which I admit is definitely a possibility, I want to be home for a while. Settle in and take over the finances at Lodge-Freeze."

Luann shook her head. "Working with family. Sounds crazy to me."

Dawn shrugged. "Not my family. We've always worked

together, and that's one of the reasons I earned the business degrees. I like numbers and making them line up."

"You sing like a star, though." Luann played with a cocktail napkin.

Dawn grinned. "I sing okay, but it's not a passion. I do that for fun." She'd never get her college buddy to understand, but she tried anyway. "Being here and working the ranches as well as the business feels right. That's my passion."

Luann snorted. "Hawk Rain is your passion, and it's more likely he'll be here than in Europe. Don't kid me."

Dawn shook her head. "Hawk and I are just friends."

Luann sighed. "Promise me you'll think about the tour. Just keep an open mind."

"I promise." Dawn nodded as Mrs. Hudson waved a card. "Looks like I'm up. Talk to you later." She left her friend and walked to the bingo table, quickly shoving the pillow out of sight. Seriously. A pillow? She had to dissuade the ladies as soon as possible, or they'd never leave her alone.

How was she going to do that?

CHAPTER 3

Fall in love with your heart, but use your brain to make sure it's right.
~ The Lady Elks Secret Archives.

THE RURAL ROAD cut between snowy fields under attack by the wind. Dawn drove her SUV slowly over the icy streets after the vigorous bingo game, her mind throwing thoughts to the forefront like scattering buckshot while Mrs. Poppins pouted in the passenger seat.

Why did the entire town have to know about her childhood crush on Hawk Rain? What would it be like to live in a big city where nobody knew her business?

Probably not fun. She'd been to college and grad school away from town, and like it or not, she'd missed everybody. It was great to be home, and once she nipped this issue with Hawk in the bud, life would be good.

"You're driving too fast, Dawn Freeze," Mrs. Poppins muttered, holding her bulging purse to her chest.

"I'm sorry." While the rural route remained empty, the roads were icy, and the storm continued to rage. Dawn slowed from thirty miles an hour to twenty. The speed limit was fifty, but Mrs. Poppins had lost at bingo, and she seemed a bit peeved.

Mrs. Hudson had won the most at bingo, and she'd all but danced out the door with Henry Bullton, whispering loudly that he was gonna *get some.* For some reason, to Mrs. Hudson, winning meant all her dreams would soon come true. Including Hawk falling for Dawn.

Dawn shook her head.

A thump alerted her, and her SUV jumped. Groaning, she pulled to the side of the very deserted country road. The Jeep slid on the ice, and she corrected until she could pull to a stop.

"Oh my goodness. Oh my goodness." Mrs. Poppins yanked off her scarf and fanned herself, her eyes wide behind her spectacles. "We hit somebody."

Dawn patted the elderly lady's knee. "We didn't hit anybody. I promise." Squinting out the window, she sucked back another groan at seeing the snow pounding down. "Feels like a flat tire." Her cell phone glowed on the seat next to her, and without a doubt she could call any of her brothers or her father to come change the tire.

Heck. Her mother and sisters-in-law could change the tire.

So could she.

Did she want to? Um, no. But it was time everyone saw her as an adult and not the Lodge-Freeze boys' little sister. Changing the tire would make her cold and irritated...but provide no danger.

Not in Maverick County.

"I'll have the tire changed in just a second, Mrs. Poppins," Dawn said, keeping her voice low and reassuring.

"No." Sharp nails dug into Dawn's arm. "Let's call for help. Right now."

Dawn patted the gnarled hand. "I can change a tire, ma'am. It'll be okay."

Mrs. Poppins rolled surprisingly bright green eyes. "Of

course you can change a tire, Dawnie. Geez. If you couldn't change a tire, you wouldn't be a girl I'd let drive me home. But what I'm saying is...you don't *need* to change the tire."

"Yes, I do." She smiled at the frowning woman.

Mrs. Poppins squinted out at the storm. "What if there are rapists out there?" She glanced down at her shimmering black pantsuit. "Patty bedazzled my shirt, and I'm rather, well, hot in this."

Amusement filled Dawn's chest, and she coughed out a laugh. "You surely are, but I doubt any rapists are trolling along this rural road in this storm. Way too cold."

Mrs. Poppins sniffed and nearly pressed her nose against the window, looking out at the storm. "If you say so."

Straightening her shoulders, Dawn slid from the car and moved to check the back tire. Yep. Flat as a pancake. Must've driven over a sharp rock not covered enough by ice.

She'd been thinking about Hawk and not watching the road.

Thinking of Hawk...he'd rescue her if she called him. Tempting. Yep. Definitely tempting. But they both deserved better than games, and they were only friends. Just like Adam. Seemed she had several hot, way too sexy men around who just wanted to be her buddy. Freakin' great.

Plus, she could change a tire.

So she jacked up the car, removed the old tire, and grunted while securing the new one. Mrs. Poppins watched carefully out the rolled down back window, her face pale and pinched. The snow turned to sleeting rain, and Dawn's face was numb by the time she finished.

Yet triumph filled her as she tossed the jack into the back of the SUV.

Country girl all the way. Feeling rather proud of herself, and definitely superior to any woman who needed saving from a silly flat tire on an icy road, she turned to head back to the driver's seat. Her boot caught a chunk of ice. Her arms windmilled while she fought gravity.

And promptly fell flat on her ass.

Her head *thunked* the metal of the SUV, and her vision swayed. Darkness danced in front of her eyes. Oh crap. Maybe she should've called for help.

She blinked several times, and her vision cleared. Good. Heck, she'd been knocked on the head before. No biggie. Then another pain made itself known in her right hand. Ouch. Cold or seriously hurt? She couldn't tell.

Mrs. Poppins scooted out the vehicle, her galoshes throwing up ice as she landed on the road. "Oh my. Oh my. Are you all right?"

Dawn wasn't sure. "I think so." Scrambling along the ice, she inched her way inside the vehicle with the elderly woman's help and shut the door before grabbing the phone. Her ears rang, and clouds danced across her eyes. "I'm not sure I should drive."

"Oh my." Mrs. Poppins bit her lip and sat back in the passenger seat again. "I drank three glasses of wine, but I could give it a shot."

Bad idea. Very. "I'll call for assistance."

"No. You relax." Mrs. Poppins grasped the phone and scrolled through her contacts. "I'll call my Earl to come get us."

Dawn stilled. "Um, how about we call my dad?" Earl was a great man, but at this time of night, he'd be into the Scotch.

"Good idea." Mrs. Poppins nodded, her concentration absolute. "There we go." She dialed and pressed the phone to her ear. "Hi dear. This is Bernie Poppins." Then she waited several beats before clearing her throat. "Well, we were heading home from bingo, and I thought Dawn hit a person, but maybe it was just a moose. Anyway, the girl got hurt." She vigorously shook her head at the response. "No need for an ambulance, but we do need a ride, at about mile marker seven on Solstice Road. Hurry up, young man." She clicked the phone shut.

Only Mrs. Poppins would dare call Tom Freeze a young man and order him to hurry up.

Dawn turned the key in the ignition and turned up the heat. Ahhh. Much better. Leaning her head back, she closed her eyes and tried to thaw.

Mrs. Poppins poked her in the side. "How's your head?"

"Good." Dawn opened her eyes. "Slight headache, but my vision is fine." She glanced down at her aching wrist. "I think I'm bruised but nothing is broken. I could probably drive us home."

"Absolutely not. I called for help." Mrs. Poppins' lips firmed.

Dawn heard what must be her dad's truck in the distance, and she sat up as he pulled to a stop behind her.

Mere seconds later, the door was wrenched open, and Hawk stood outside, his green eyes darker than normal. He wore faded jeans and a dark T-shirt, and his shoulder length black hair looked ruffled, like he'd been asleep. The guy hadn't bothered to grab a jacket, and snow quickly covered his broad shoulders.

"You okay?" he asked.

She tried to focus. "Where's my dad?"

Hawk stepped closer and brought the scent of darkened forest with him. "Are. You. Okay?" Fire now burned in his eyes, and his jaw worked in what looked like anger.

Scary. Hawk on the side of the road in an irritated mood was actually kind of...scary. "I'm freakin' fine. Where's my dad?"

Mrs. Poppins twittered. "Oh my. I got the phone numbers mixed up."

Dread slithered down to land in Dawn's abdomen. Embarrassment followed quickly. She turned a look on her companion. "You didn't."

Mrs. Poppins grinned, showing her perfectly spaced dentures. "Oops."

Dawn could swear a growl rumbled from Hawk's muscled chest as he leaned in, his body way too close.

"Babe? If you don't answer my question—"

She turned to face him. A tingle spread through her abdomen, reaching and warming her private parts. Now that was a voice she wouldn't mind hearing late at night under the covers. Sexy, dangerous, and masculine.

Unfortunately, also impatient...and sliding rapidly to pissed off, if she had to guess. She sighed. "I'm fine. Hit my head and landed on my wrist. Stop being scary and go away."

Mrs. Poppins clucked her tongue. "She didn't mean that. Must be the brain injury."

Dawn leaned forward and rested her head on the steering wheel. "I can't do this. I really can't take this—not now. Please. No list, no meddling, no mistaken phone calls. Please."

Mrs. Poppins patted her arm. "See? She's delirious."

Hawk clasped Dawn at the base of the neck and drew her gently back. His hand was firm and warm, determined. A shiver wandered right down her spine, and his hold tightened.

Oh man. He'd felt the shiver.

Then his face was in hers, separated by a mere inch.

Her breath caught, and the universe stopped moving. Completely. She focused on his forest-green eyes to keep from looking down at those full lips. *Don't look. Don't look.*

"Head injury?" he rumbled, his gaze penetrating hers. He looked deep, and he looked hard, and the hand at her nape didn't relent.

"No," she croaked out. "Little head bump...nothing to worry about." Why was it so hard to breathe all of a sudden? If he didn't back up, she was going to completely humiliate herself and flatten his butt on the icy road. It'd be worth it just to feel that impossibly hard body against hers for a few seconds.

He lifted an eyebrow. "Blink."

She huffed and blinked several times. "I'm okay."

"Your pupils look all right." He leaned in a bit more. "Seeing stars? Blurry vision?"

"No." She wanted to burrow into his heat, so she kept perfectly still. "I've had a concussion before, and I know what it feels like. This is just a bump." She'd been bucked off horses her entire life, and she knew she was fine.

Hawk rubbed the nape of her neck, and she couldn't help the small whimper.

That quickly, his face lost all sense of irritation. Something else replaced it...something heated and all male. "Let me see your wrist," he whispered, releasing her.

She couldn't take it if he touched her like that again, so she handed over her wrist.

He gently clasped her arm and turned it this way and that in the light from the car. "Bruised."

"I know." She gingerly retracted her arm. "I'm fine."

"No she isn't." Mrs. Poppins clucked her tongue.

Hawk straightened and glanced around the quiet road. "You didn't hit a moose."

"Of course not." Dawn shook her head and then winced as pain cut into the back of her eyes. "It was just a flat tire."

"Okay." Hawk rubbed his chin then slowly drew her from the car to open the rear door and place her in the backseat. "Let's take Mrs. Poppins home, and then we'll figure out what to do with you." Without waiting for an answer, he secured Dawn's seat belt, shut the door, and slid into the driver's seat. Seconds later, he pushed the seat back and drove onto the road.

Mrs. Poppins bounced happily against her seat belt. "She shouldn't be alone, you know. Just in case it's a concussion. Could be."

Hawk glanced into the rear view mirror. "She won't be alone. I promise."

CHAPTER 4

All men are heroes. They just might need a nudge. ~ The Lady Elks
Secret Archives.

HAWK DIDN'T LIKE SURPRISES, he didn't like storms, and he sure
didn't like Dawn wounded on the side of the road in a blizzard.

Come to think of it...he didn't like much of anything these
days.

The second the call had come in, he'd jumped into clothes
and rushed to his truck. If anything happened to the blue-eyed
temptress, he'd cut off his own head.

As he pulled up in front of the Poppins' farmhouse, he swallowed an expletive at the snow-covered front walk that led up
to the sprawling ranch house surrounded by acres of fields and
forest. While the storm had been brutal all day, the walk should
have about six inches of snow...not three feet. "Where's Earl?"

Mrs. Poppins gingerly stepped out the SUV. "Inside. The fool
hurt his back last week and won't let me call the boys for help."

Hawk jumped out of the SUV and hustled to reach for Mrs.

Poppins' arm. As the old lady stumbled in the thick snow, he smoothly lifted her up.

"Oh my." She giggled and patted his chest, her hand so light he barely felt it. "You are a strong one, Hawk Rain." A very amusing rosy blush wound just under the paper-thin skin in her cheeks.

He glanced back toward the car and waited until Dawn unrolled her window. "You okay for a few minutes?"

She nodded, her face pale.

"Get in the front and keep the heat running." He waited with supreme patience for her to exit the car and slide into the front seat. She moved easily and with grace.

Good. She was all right.

Then he carefully carried Mrs. Poppins through the thick snow and into her front vestibule where he reached for the ever-present shovel leaning against a coat rack. The smell of apple pie and lemon cleanser surrounded them.

She twittered. "Oh, Hawk. You don't have to—"

He grinned. "Just give me a second, Mrs. P." He'd given her the nickname at the age of ten when she'd smacked him over the head with a spoon after he'd stolen apples from her orchard. Then she'd promptly baked him a pie and made sure he ate it before sending him home.

Turning, he dug deep into the snow and had the walk clear within a few minutes. The Poppins kids had moved to Billings, and he would give them a call the next morning. They were good guys and had probably just not realized their folks needed help.

Returning to the house, he put the shovel back in place.

Mrs. Poppins leaned up and kissed him on the cheek. "Take care of our Dawnie, would you?"

"Of course." He shut the door and strode toward the car to fold into the driver's seat. Once back on the road, he turned toward the too-silent woman. "How's your head?"

"Fine." Dawn crossed her arms over her chest.

"Good." He concentrated on the road and tried to ignore her scent—all woman, all sweet huckleberry. "Where am I taking you?"

She pivoted in her seat, both eyebrows arching. "Home."

Ah. He hadn't been clear. "It's highly doubtful, but there's a very small chance you have a concussion, Dawnie. Local rules are nobody stays alone after hitting their head. Choose a place to go."

"Home." She ground out the word between gritted teeth.

He hadn't hauled ass into a freezing blizzard to drop her off alone at home, and the woman wasn't getting him. Not at all. "You can go to your folks or to any of your brothers' homes. So choose." No way was he dropping her at Adam's.

"No. Take me home." She hunched down in her seat and pouted like she had when he and Colton had refused to take her riding when they were teenagers.

His temper tickled the base of his neck, so he tried reason. "What's the problem?"

She sighed. "Listen, Hawk. I get where you're coming from, but I need to go home. If I run to my family every time something goes wonky, then they'll never take me seriously. I'm having enough problems."

He slowed the car over a particularly icy spot. "What are you talking about?"

Her slim shoulders hunched forward even more. "None of your business."

That cut a little deeper than he would've expected, and he reacted before thinking. "Oh, baby, that is not how this is going down." The girl had a softness to her that had always concerned him, so he pulled the car onto the shoulder and shoved the gearshift into neutral to better reason with her. "What the fuck is going on?"

Her gaze lashed to his, blue and widened.

"Yeah. I said fuck." He half turned toward her, his temper unraveling too quickly to tie back up. "You're all grown up now, singing in a bar, working at the company...and you don't want your family's help. So yeah. I'm done holding back."

He raised an eyebrow and pierced her with a look that had once made a junior soldier nearly piss his pants. So when Dawn rolled her eyes, his head jerked.

She sniffed. "You're cranky tonight."

Cranky? Did she just say *cranky* like he was old Earl Poppins? "Then you shouldn't have called for my help," he ground out.

"I didn't call for your help. Mrs. Poppins did."

Hawk scratched his jaw. "Yeah. About that."

"I'm not talking about that. Period." Dawn leaned back and crossed her arms. "I'm sure she meant to call Colton and accidentally dialed you."

The woman couldn't lie worth a damn. Hawk reached out and grasped her chin, slowly pulling her around to face him. "Bullshit."

Pink rose into her face, and his fingers actually warmed. Two seconds later, his cock hardened. Could he warm her up like that everywhere? His gaze dropped to her pretty lips.

She was too much of a temptation, and he'd never been one to ignore a challenge. To finally be home, to be near her, to have her all but throwing down the gauntlet?

Yeah. No way was he strong enough to turn that off. He couldn't get the image of Adam squiring her away out of his mind, which was why he'd been tossing and turning when the distress call had come in.

One taste. He just wanted one little taste. So he leaned over and wrapped one arm around her waist, lifted, and settled her ass in his lap.

She gurgled—actually gurgled—and settled against him, her fingers curling into his T-shirt. "Wh-what are you doing?"

He leaned in to make sure he had her full attention. "I'm going to kiss you, and then we're going to agree which house you're going to tonight—pick a brother or your folks."

She swallowed, and her gaze dropped to his lips. "K-kiss me?"

"Yep." Amusement filtered through him along with lust. She was adorable and sweet.

Her gaze lifted to his. "Wh-why?"

"Because I want to." Sometimes, it was as simple as that. He'd take a taste, prove to them both that it was nothing special, and then move on.

Even at the thought, he knew he was a liar. For once, he didn't care. Not right now. Seeing her leave with Adam the other night had created a slow burn inside Hawk that he couldn't extinguish.

So he leaned in and brushed her mouth with his.

Soft. So amazingly soft.

She murmured something against his lips. What, he didn't know. But his hand moved on its own to her nape, beneath all that thick hair—pure silk a guy could get lost in forever.

He was tired of fighting, and he was tired of wishing. Most of all, he was tired of wondering. So he held her in place and delved deep.

Heaven. Pure and simple...huckleberry-flavored heaven.

She sighed against him, her mouth opening, her body leaning into his. Her nails dug into his chest, and the small pain ignited something in him. Something new.

Careful to keep her away from the steering wheel, Hawk twisted his torso, shoved the seat all the way back, and smoothly swung her around to straddle him. The second her core hit his pounding cock, he groaned.

She tunneled her hands into his hair, and a soft moan echoed up from her chest.

He'd known. He'd known if he ever touched her, she'd burn

him. Dawn Freeze was all in—no matter what she did. Now, she was all into him.

And it felt great.

He released her neck to run both palms down her sides, settling them at her waist. She tilted against him, and the blood rushed through his head and directly south.

Finally, she broke their connection and leaned back. She swallowed several times and then exhaled slowly. "Um, ah, I'll go to my brother Quinn's house."

Hawk blinked.

In the darkness, her luminous eyes glowed. Her tongue flicked her lips, and her panting breath rasped. Her thick mass of hair had been mussed, giving her a look he'd like to see in the morning. With a soft pat to his chest, Dawn scooted off him to settle in the passenger seat. "Okay?"

Hawk let her go, his mind flaring fully awake. "Quinn's?"

"Yes." Dawn reached for the seat belt, her gaze on the storm. "Colton and Melanie have babies coming and need sleep. Jake and Sophie already have a new baby boy as well as Leila and Nathan, so if they're sleeping, I'm not gonna wake them up. So it's Quinn and Juliet. They're probably trying to make a baby, considering the rest of the family wants them to, but surely they're done for the night."

Why had she stopped? Hawk shook his head. He wouldn't have pushed it beyond a kiss or two, but honestly? He figured *he* would've had to pull back, especially since she might have a headache. The last thing he'd ever do was manhandle her while she was hurt. "Are you in love with Adam?"

Dawn turned toward him. "*Now* you ask that?"

He exhaled slowly to fight both temper and guilt. "Yeah. Now I ask that. You answer it."

"Man, you're bossy." She turned toward the window in what he could only term as a huff. "Mind your own business."

"Considering my tongue was halfway down your throat a second ago, this *is* my business." He put the vehicle in drive and pulled onto the road. "Besides. You've always been my business, and you know it."

"Not anymore. Not since you told me to screw off after Colt's wedding." No hurt, only matter-of-factness, existed in Dawn's tone. Which clearly meant he *had* hurt her.

"I never said any such thing." The woman was so dramatic sometimes. "I just said that I was leaving, and when I came back, if I came back, we were just friends." Truth be told, he would've bet against his surviving, and leaving her as a friend had seemed kinder.

Her head turned so quickly her hair fanned out. "Then you should've kept your tongue in your own mouth tonight, right?"

That was exactly right, and he knew it. "You kissed me back."

"So?" She lifted one slim shoulder. "After all these years, I was curious. Now I'm not."

A grin flew to his face unbidden. She'd always challenged him, and this was just one more poke from the brat. He'd learned his lesson after breaking his arm when she'd dared him to swing past the boulders in Miller's Pond, and he'd landed hard. "Sure you are."

Her chin slowly lifted. "You're an arrogant ass, Hawk Rain. I'm glad we're just friends."

For some reason, her temper cooled his. Good thing, too. "I shouldn't have kissed you, Dawnie." The girl was smart to stay away from him, and he should be happy for her and Adam. Even though Adam was too old for her. "Don't be mad at me."

"I'm not." She huffed and turned toward her window.

Sure she wasn't. He sighed. After a good night's sleep, he'd figure out a way to get things back on track.

They drove through the blizzard to Quinn's house, a two-story ranch house with newly painted shutters and a wrap-around porch. Perfectly spaced Christmas lights glittered along all the eaves. Hawk whistled.

Dawn grinned, peering out at the colorful display. "Juliet really gets into Christmas, and she made my brother fix the lights seven times. Quinn didn't used to be so patient, right?"

Definitely not. Quinn and Jake Lodge were the closest thing Hawk had to older brothers, and neither had ever been patient. Their mom had married Tom Freeze and then had Colton and Dawn, and once Hawk's mom had died, they'd enfolded him like family.

Which was yet another reason he couldn't date Dawn. Talk about losing everybody if it didn't work out—which it wouldn't. Not now, and not until he got his head back on straight and could learn to relax and just enjoy life without looking for a threat around every corner. If he ever could get to that point, which sometimes he doubted.

Dawn opened the door and hopped down to the snowy driveway. "I'll wake Quinn to let him know I'm here and why. Thanks for the rescue tonight, and I'll get my rig back from you sometime tomorrow." She slammed the door and ran for the front porch, her hair catching snowflakes.

Instant silence and suffocating loneliness settled in the truck. Hawk stiffened his shoulders and waited until Dawn had dug in her purse for a key to open the front door. She waved before slipping inside, and he lifted a hand to wave back.

Then, his body heavy, he turned her SUV toward home. He'd need to get a ranch hand out to grab his truck once the blizzard died down.

About halfway home, his phone buzzed. "Yeah?" he answered.

"Hawk? It's Deputy Phillips. We found your truck on the side of Solstice Road. You okay?"

Only in Mineral Lake did everyone have everyone else's cell

phone numbers. "Yeah, Fred. I'm fine. Dawn Freeze had a flat tire, fixed it, and I drove her to Quinn's house in her rig."

"Oh, good. Want me to call Buck out and get your truck towed?"

Hawk slowed down to avoid a chunk of ice in the middle of the road. "Nah, let Buck sleep." The retired football coach had just recuperated from a triple bypass. Thanks to Dawn's letters, Hawk was mostly up on the town happenings. "In fact, the spare keys are in the middle console, if you could do me a solid."

"Sure thing. Jack is with me. We'll just drop your truck off at your ranch for ya. Quiet night," Fred said.

Hawk grinned. "That's mighty kind of you. Thanks."

"No problem. I hadn't heard that Dawnie was house-sitting for the sheriff. We'll make sure to patrol around there at night until he gets home," Fred said.

Hawk stilled. "Quinn's out of town?"

"Yep. He and Juliet are taking a long weekend in Billings. Didn't ya know?" Fred asked.

"Nope." Which is exactly why the brat had agreed to go to Quinn's. She had probably borrowed a rig and was halfway home. With a possible concussion. "Bye, Phillips." Hawk hung up and flipped a U-turn.

He and Dawn Freeze were about to have a discussion about lying and playing games. She might be savvy, but he was pissed.

She should've taken the reprieve. He'd tried to be a good guy, tried to be honorable. In fact, he'd let her leave, with his body still on fire for her. If she wanted to throw down such a dare, he was more than ready, and there was no question the woman knew what she was doing. She'd kissed him back, full on, and she'd been breathing as heavily as he'd been when they'd finished.

Her shrug and casual request to go to her brother's had almost masked the challenge in her eyes.

She knew he was arrogant, and she knew full well he'd pick up that challenge. In fact, he'd bet his last dollar she'd be waiting on her porch. So he could turn around and go home, or he could see just how much of him she could really handle. She wanted to play games? Fine.

He hadn't lost one yet.

CHAPTER 5

Men are smarter than horses...probably. ~ The Lady Elks Secret Archives.

DAWN CHUCKLED. Hawk should've known better than to try the "I'm the boss" move with her. Would he have kept kissing her if she hadn't stopped them? Part of her had wanted to continue on to definite orgasmic bliss, and the other part had just plain and simply freaked out. He kissed better than she'd imagined, and she'd imagined some amazing things. All of a sudden, she hadn't been in control.

Fire lived in Hawk Rain, and she needed time to think. Time to let her body calm down. Time to cool off so his heat didn't end up destroying her.

She had feelings for him, and there was no denying her body was primed and ready for him. But it wasn't just about them. Her family mattered, and Hawk's friendship with Colton was too important to harm. Also, Hawk wasn't home for good yet. He had one eye on the door, even while he'd been drinking with

Colt at the bar. So she would take some alone time to mull things over.

Plus, Hawk had gotten all bossy, and she couldn't allow him to get away with it. Once he'd left her at Quinn's, she'd borrowed Juliet's SUV to go home. *Take that, bossy pants.*

Mirth filled her as she pulled the Jeep into the driveway of her cabin. Well, it was Colton's cabin, but he'd moved into Mel's house when they got married, and the cabin fit Dawn perfectly. Especially after she'd deep-cleaned the place. A frozen stream wound behind the back porch while trees spread out all around, giving the sense of privacy and comfort.

She turned off the ignition and jumped out just as *her* SUV lumbered down the main drive of the sprawling ranch. The bright lights cut through the night. Crap. How had Hawk figured it out so quickly? Or maybe he hadn't, and he'd returned to Quinn's in order to finish what they'd started in the truck and then followed her? She sucked in a deep breath, having expected at least a little reprieve before he picked up the challenge she'd definitely tossed down.

From the way he was speeding toward her house, she suspected his arrival had less to do with that get-some gauntlet and more to do with her purposely deceiving him. Hawk in full temper was never pretty, and he'd already been pissed off at finding her in a blizzard. He wouldn't take kindly to her lying to him as well. Ducking her head, she hustled toward the covered front porch and waited.

No way would she run.

Hawk skidded to a stop and was out of the SUV in record time. Barreling through the storm, he came right at her, emerald eyes blazing. Even with snow billowing around him, he prowled like a determined panther on the hunt, graceful and deadly. And seriously pissed.

Well, geez. Talk about overreacting. She lifted her chin. "Hawk—"

"No." He stepped into her and kept right on going.

Yelping, she grabbed his shoulders as he lifted her and clamped both hands on her ass. Seconds later, her back hit the door. Not hard, but not gentle, either.

She gasped. "What—"

"Where's the key?" he ground out, his face in hers.

"Not locked." Her heart battered her rib cage, and her breath caught.

He raised an eyebrow and opened the door. "Why isn't it locked?"

She frowned. "Seriously? We're on the main ranch—my parents live north, my brothers in every direction. We don't lock any doors unless we're out of town."

His face hardened.

Oops.

"Like Quinn is right now?" Hawk shoved through the door and kicked it shut behind him, rattling a picture of the Eiffel Tower on the wall. The small Christmas tree she'd already put up shook in the corner.

"Um—" she whispered.

He leaned into her face, his breath fanning her lips. "Quinn's Christmas lights threw me."

"They're on a timer." She shoved against Hawk, getting nowhere. "If you're so worried about my head, shouldn't you take it easy?"

"Does your head hurt?" he asked.

"No," she admitted.

"Then you're fine but I'm not leaving you alone, just in case." He held her easily, impressive muscles rippling in his chest.

She swallowed as parts of her heated throughout her body. "Put me down."

Amusement—too dark to make her comfortable—glittered in his eyes. "You wanted to play, Dawnie. Now we play," he whispered.

The tone, low and masculine, echoed in her torso, zinged around, and zapped right down to her core. She'd imagined this. Kind of. The reality of Hawk held more intensity, more danger, than she'd expected.

But she liked danger, right?

"You're sending mixed messages," she murmured, her gaze dropping to his mouth. But man, she liked how he felt.

His hands clenched on her butt, and his mouth hovered right over hers. "How is this a mixed message?"

She bit her lip. It was difficult to misread his intent. Even so, how could this be happening? To have a moment that she'd so longed for finally come was almost unbelievable. Yet she was fully awake. This *was* happening. "I don't understand."

"You in love with Adam?" he asked.

That again? "No," she whispered. "Just friends."

Hawk's chin lifted. "That's not what it looked like."

"I know," she admitted.

His gaze darkened. "I'm not a guy you play games with, baby."

She shrugged. "Not playing—never was." How many times had she dreamed about being in Hawk's arms? Sure, her fantasies were a bit more "swept off her feet" than "up against a wall," but even so. Nothing came close to the reality.

The reality thundered through her, springing every nerve alive and wide-awake. She reached out and slid her hand along his cut jaw. Stubble tickled her palm. "This is crazy."

"I know. Let's be crazy." He lowered his head. "I'm only home the week, and you gotta know that. Say yes."

"Whoa." She wanted him with every cell in her body. "You can't just change your mind like that."

He chuckled. "My mind hasn't changed. This is a bad idea. I know it's a bad idea, but I'm tired of fighting it. Seeing you leave with Adam shot a rock into my gut, and I've been thinking since. Obviously not clearly, but who the hell cares. I'm done holding back."

She shivered at his husky tone. Hawk in a thinking mood rarely boded well. "And?"

"And you're gonna find somebody else at some point. If not Adam, then a lucky bastard who'll get you for the rest of his life." Hawk lowered his forehead to hers in a curiously gentle gesture. "I know it can't be me. Not with my job, and not with the next mission. But I have a week, and you're all grown up, Dawn."

Yeah. She was all grown up, and it was about time he saw her that way. A sadness she couldn't ignore echoed in his words. "You'll come home for good someday, right?"

"I don't know." He remained tense beneath her touch, so solid it hurt. "I made a promise, and in keeping it, I probably won't make it home. But we have this week, and I want it. For the future, to always remember. We're safe here at home for now, and I'm done fighting it. I'm done fighting you." He leaned back, his gaze heated. "Say yes. This is your decision, Dawnie."

"Yes," she breathed. Forget consequences. This? Yeah. This she wanted. She'd played it safe her entire life, not really having much choice with three overprotective brothers around. Safe was for wusses. She'd worry about repercussions tomorrow. After.

"You sure?" Hawk asked.

For an answer, she shot both hands into his thick hair and planted her lips on his. Not hard...but not exactly gentle, either.

He growled low, his mouth overtaking hers, all heated male.

Hawk Rain could kiss. Within two seconds, any doubts Dawn had disappeared. Completely. Yes, he could kiss that well. Rumors had abounded in high school, and they were all true.

She moaned deep in her throat, her nipples pebbling hard enough to hurt.

He stepped back, his tongue working hers, and then turned

for the bedroom. Her coat hit the floor, followed by her shirt. It happened so quickly, she didn't even realize he'd had to stop kissing her to get the cotton off—his mouth was that fast to return to hers.

Her bra came next, and the second her back hit the bed, her boots, jeans, and panties disappeared, as if just by thinking it, Hawk could get her naked.

Impressive. And kind of breathtaking, with a side of worry.

He finally released her mouth to stand and tug his snow-wet shirt over his head.

Whoa.

She'd seen Hawk in swim shorts, and she'd seen him running with Colton. His chest wasn't unfamiliar. But in the years they'd been apart, he'd grown broad and strong...and ripped. Seriously ripped.

A knife wound and what looked like bullet wounds were scattered across his torso and down his abdomen. His jeans hit the floor next, and she forgot to breathe. *All* of the rumors were true—he was definitely gifted.

He leaned a knee on the bed and then was on her. Full frontal, Hawk Rain, all hard angles and smooth strength...on her. Tingles shook through her, and she smiled. "I've wondered."

"Me, too." His mouth dipped to her collarbone, and he traced a path down to kiss the underside of her breast. His hands were busier than his mouth, skimming her sides, stroking down her flanks, sliding around her butt.

With a shift of muscle, he turned, and she found herself on top of him, straddling him.

"Better," he murmured, his hands going to her breasts. "You're beautiful, Dawnie."

His touch was one thing—the reverent words another. At his tone, something in her loosened. She relaxed and slid right into the moment she'd always dreamed about.

She flattened her hands against his chest, a soft purr

escaping her. His skin was darker than hers and covered so much strength. For so long, she'd wanted to touch him. No matter what happened the next morning, she was taking the chance. "I love your chest," she said, curling in her fingers.

He tweaked her nipple. "Yours is better."

Liquid shot to her thighs, and she couldn't help pressing down on his hard shaft. Shock ricocheted through her, and she threw back her head to grind harder.

"Slow down," he whispered, his free hand rolling her other nipple.

"Can't." She fell forward to slide her mouth along his jaw.

Her only warning was a *whoosh* of sound before he manacled her waist—again—and rolled them over.

"Then you're done on top." He levered himself up on one arm to keep from crushing her and swept his free hand down between her breasts, over her abs, and straight for home.

"Control freak," she muttered widening her legs, caressing down his sides.

"You have no idea, but you're about to learn." Then he slid one finger inside her.

She gasped, electrical zaps convulsing her sex. "I don't like bossy, Hawk." If nothing else, she knew how to get to him.

"Too bad." He shifted down her torso, licking and nipping, his mouth soon finding her mound. "For years, you've done whatever you wanted... sometimes dangerously and often foolishly. I've tried reason, I've tried friendship, and I've even tried asking nicely. Now...now we're gonna try something else." To further make his point, he slid another finger inside her and sucked her entire clit into his mouth.

That quickly—she shattered. Crying out his name, she arched into his mouth and let the firestorm consume her. The orgasm whipped through her with such energy all she could do was close her eyes and ride out the riptide.

His smile held no small amount of determination as he

maneuvered back up her body. "You're gorgeous when you let go."

She reached down and grasped him, sliding her palm along his length. "We can go slow later."

"Fair enough." He grabbed a foil packet out of his jeans, bit it open, and unrolled it with steady hands. With masculine grace, he positioned himself at her entrance and began to ease in. Slow and careful.

Tears sparked the back of her eyes. Even now, even in the moment of passion edged with pain, he was careful with her. Finally, he pushed gently all the way home.

She arched, surprise mingling with a dark pleasure inside her. He was too much. So much. Her orgasm had prepared her somewhat, but even so, there was a lot to Hawk. And all of him was inside her.

She brushed dark hair off his forehead, suddenly consumed with more than lust. More than need. "Hawk."

Tenderness mixed with the desire glittering in his eyes, and he brushed his thumb across her lower lip. "I know."

Yeah.

They were joined. Completely, absolutely, male to female, and it was better than she'd ever hoped it would be. She smiled and ran a hand down his back to his smooth butt. "I've always admired your rear, you know. It's phenomenal."

He grinned. "Right back at you." Then he pulled out and thrust back in. A muscle ticked in his jaw, showing the corded strength down his neck. "You're tight, sweetheart."

She wrapped her legs around his hips and her arms around his shoulders. "Slow later. Fast now."

He shook loose of her arms until she dropped back onto the pillow. "Fine. Slow later. But you give me your eyes."

Now, that was intimate, and she wasn't quite sure she could handle it. He'd used that voice...the one that meant he'd issued an order and would wait until she gave in. So she stared directly into his eyes. "Fine. Let's see what you've got."

His grin held so much promise, a tremble vibrated through her. His grin widened.

Securing her hip and lifting her partially from the bed, he started to thrust, hard, strong, and so deep she had no clue where he ended and she began. He took all of her, and he did it fast, furious, and with finality.

She'd worry about that later.

For now, she could only feel. Every nerve in her body flared and hungered. The harder he thrust, the tighter he held her, the freer she felt. Wildness lived in her and always had. For once, Hawk was there with her—far more wild than she'd ever be.

He reached down and encircled her clit with two fingers.

She gasped, her body stilling, her breath catching.

Then he pinched.

Her entire being climaxed. No slow uncoil, no slow burn, she just exploded into flames. Her eyes rolled back, she dug her fingers into his butt, and she let oblivion take her away. He'd keep her safe.

Waves, somehow sharp and pummeling, rippled through her, tightening every muscle into absolute bliss. She rode it out, holding him, coming down with a whimper. The orgasm finally waned, and he thrust harder, lifting her higher. The spiral snapped closed again, and her mouth opened in a silent scream. The next orgasm shook her to her core, taking everything. She held on with all her strength, holding firm, her body shaking head to toe.

Finally, she came down.

"Eyes," he growled.

She swallowed, her eyes drifting open to see determination and promise in his. His hold somehow tightened, and he pistoned hard, his gaze keeping hers. The second he went over, her heart seized.

She exhaled slowly as he ground against her and came. Finally, he kissed her with so much tenderness, tears sprang to her eyes.

Hawk Rain. Finally.

He rolled off her and turned her to face him before sliding her hair out of her eyes. "You okay?" he asked.

"Great." She played with his chest, her gaze dropping, shyness suddenly swamping her.

"Eyes, baby."

She glanced up.

"No hiding. Period," he said.

Fine. He wanted to talk? Well, she could chat with the best of them, and she had questions. "You were angry, and I've seen you do some things in temper, but this was a change of heart. A big one. What's going on?"

He leaned into her touch. "I'm tired of fighting, Dawnie." He turned and brushed her fingers with a soft kiss. "Honestly? Seeing you leave with Adam turned me around. I didn't like it."

"Adam and I are just friends," she whispered, stretching.

"I know." Hawk angled toward her, his hand wrapping around her hip. "Someday you'll be more than that with somebody. Maybe Adam, maybe not. The idea makes something hurt deep inside me."

For Hawk Rain, that was about as close to a declaration of love as Dawn had ever heard. The guy had been head over heels for a track star in high school, and even then he hadn't professed that much emotion.

Dawn flattened her hand against his chest. "So you're saying there's a chance."

He grinned at the *Dumb and Dumber* reference. "I'm only here a week. If I get the job done next time, then we'll talk when I get back."

She shook her head. "You don't sound like you're going to make it back."

He sighed. "Can't talk about it, but it's dangerous, and I signed on."

A chill ticked through her. "You don't have to do everything alone."

"This, I do. We have a week, Dawn. Take it or don't." His voice remained level, but fire, pure and green, lit his unique eyes. Even so, his caress down her arm was gentle and held a sweet promise.

Her stomach quivered. "I'll take the week. Just between us, though. We keep all of this between us."

He stilled. "I'm not lying to Colton."

"Not lying, just not sharing." She shook her head. "This is special between us this week. If you come back, if I wait for you, which I'm not saying I will, and we decide to start up again? Then we'll talk about going public. For now, I want something just for us." He had to understand that after growing up in Mineral Lake.

His gaze dropped to her lips. "All right. We'll explore this, and see where we are, but I don't like lying to my best friend."

At his acquiescence, something eased in Dawn. "Works for me." Leaning forward, she pressed her lips against his. "Now, I think I owe you an orgasm."

"Not keeping score here...but if I were, you'd owe me two." He grinned.

Fair enough. Nobody ever said Dawn Freeze didn't pay her debts.

CHAPTER 6

Men and bulls, the two toughest and most stubborn creatures on earth, can't resist a challenge. ~ The Lady Elks Secret Archives.

HAWK DREW on his jeans as the most beautiful girl he'd ever seen slept quietly behind him. He should be pissed at himself, but he couldn't find the energy to draw up anger. He'd awoken Dawn a few times during the night, just to check her injuries. Man, it had been fun waking her up.

Her head was just fine…as was the rest of her.

Dawn Freeze, the girl he'd wanted for a decade, had just taken his heart and made it hers. Turning, he spent a moment enjoying the sight of her. She lay on her stomach, dark hair splayed down her smooth back. The sheet covered her legs enough that only the tops of the perfect twin globes of her butt were visible.

Yeah. The woman's ass was better than he had imagined, and he had a heck of an imagination.

He glanced around her bedroom. It was all feminine, with mint greens and whites, and the antique furniture looked familiar. It had probably been in Loni's house at some point. Wind buffeted against the closed windows, and he made a mental note to stoke the fire in the main room before he left.

Dawn's face was turned to the side and half visible. Angled features, definitely Freeze features, but delicate to the point of being fragile. Sweetness surrounded her in her abandonment to sleep.

What now?

After the previous night, he would never get her out of his system. Taking the week with her was a colossal mistake, for both of them, but he couldn't turn back now. He wouldn't. So the only practical move was to finish the job and get his life together to be good enough, strong enough, to take care of her if he survived.

Padding barefoot out of the bedroom, he shut the door and crossed the cozy living room with the pretty Christmas tree, making for the wide open kitchen. Dawn had painted the walls a cheery yellow that brought out sparkles in the dark green granite countertops. A plate of homemade cookies sat on the counter. He ate three before he found the ground coffee in the correct cupboard. His phone buzzed, and he yanked it from his pocket to answer. "Yeah?"

"Hawk? It's Reese."

Hawk stilled. "I'm taking a week off, Reese. I caught Meyer and will take down the rest of the organization after one week off." While he liked the ex-DEA guy, Hawk was only temporarily going back to hunting people. If he survived, he owned a demanding ranch and a couple of martial arts gyms, and that was going to be a good life. "Unless you're calling because you wanna visit Mineral Lake, I'm hanging up."

"Meyer escaped our transport to the federal authorities this morning," Reese returned evenly.

Hawk sagged against the counter, and lava lashed through his head, burning the back of his eyeballs. "Say that again." His

voice rolled from a lazy rumble to primal hardness as he let go
of the peaceful morning.

"Apparently Meyer had more friends on the outside than we
knew. They used road bombs and blew the van wide open
before knocking out three of my men. We've tracked him as far
as Mexico," Reese said.

Forget Mexico. Meyer was smart enough to run for a
country that would refuse to hand him over. "Are your men all
right?"

"They were just fine until I got a hold of them." Reese's voice
hardened.

"Damn it, Reese. I kept my promise to Chancy when I put
Meyer away, and now I have to do it again?" Hawk snapped. If
the escape had happened once Meyer had been in federal
custody, it wouldn't be his problem.

One week. One week of trying to live normal before he
finished the job of dismantling Meyer's little drug cartel.
Normal with the girl who'd had his heart for so long. Was it
really too much to ask?

As if on cue, she slipped into the room, her hair mussed, her
cheeks rosy, looking like a woman who'd been well loved the
night before. Several times.

Hawk froze, and an iron fist gripped his heart.

What had he done, sleeping with her before he'd been free of
his promises?

Papers shuffled over the line. "I have a series of videos and
some intel I want to run by you, and I'd prefer to do it in person.
Give me a short time to get ready, and I'll head your way," Reese
muttered.

"I want a detailed update in thirty minutes," Hawk growled
into the phone before disconnecting the call. Nausea spiraled in
his belly.

"Morning," Dawn whispered, her gaze roving to the too

quiet coffeemaker. She'd pulled on a girly, flowered robe and belted it tight, showcasing her phenomenal body.

Hawk exhaled slowly. "Morning."

His tone must've alerted her, because her blue gaze slashed back to him. "Hawk?"

First things first. "How's your wrist?" he asked.

She extended her arm and twisted back and forth. "A little sore, but not too bad."

Good. "Your head?" he asked, keeping his tone level.

"Perfectly fine." She tilted her head in clear question.

His mind spun with possible scenarios. They couldn't be together for an entire week. They'd never be able to keep it a secret—not in Mineral Lake or even in Maverick County. If anybody found out, they'd know he loved her and deserted her, and she'd be left behind to face the gossip. There was no way to know when he'd be back, and he didn't want to subject Dawn to that. "This was a mistake," he said, trying for honesty.

One of her dark eyebrows arched, and her small hands went to her hips. "You have got to be kidding me."

"I'm not," he whispered. "Last night meant the world to me, Dawnie, but it can't happen again." Not until he caught Chuck Meyer—*again*—and made sure the sociopath stood trial for running drugs while working as a soldier in the military. Hawk had trusted the justice system to deal with Meyer once, and it had screwed him. Time for him to do what Hawk did best— track, hunt, and drop the bastard in a cell himself.

Dawn rolled her eyes and exhaled heavily. "Why can't last night happen again?"

Now that was the question, wasn't it? "I can't tell you." Steeling his back, leaning back against the granite counter, Hawk prepared for an explosive display of temper.

Slowly, deliberately, Dawn lifted one toned shoulder. "Okay."

He blinked and half shook his head. "Okay? Really?"

"Yep." She pushed unruly hair out of her eyes. "I stopped chasing you a long time ago, Hawk. You want to be here? Then be here. You want to run away, feel free to get those legs pumping. But know this—I'm not waiting for you to figure out what you want."

His temper stirred, because what he wanted stood in front of him, full of defiance, irritation, and a hurt she was trying to mask. "You don't understand," he murmured.

"Don't care to." She turned to leave the room. "See you later."

Two strides across the kitchen had him grabbing her arm and twirling her around. "See you later? That's it? Last night didn't do a thing for you?" he asked.

The smile lifting her lips held enough mockery to boil his blood. "Sure. I've been curious for years, and you're a great fuck. I figured you would be. If that's all you wanted, then congrats… you got it. But hey, I did enjoy myself." Eyes sparking, she stood on her tiptoes to get closer to his face. "Don't let the door hit your ass on the way out. Especially since I believe my bite marks are still there."

A great fuck? He reacted without an ounce of thought, pushing her up against the kitchen wall. Going on total instinct, he crushed his mouth against hers, trying to drive those words back down her throat.

The night before, he'd taken her with more gentleness than he'd thought he had inside him, but in that moment, he forgot kindness.

Now, pissed off beyond belief, he kissed her so hard she'd taste him for a week—branding her, claiming her, showing her that one little shoulder shrug and dismissal wouldn't work. She tasted like huckleberries and woman, and in two seconds, he was lost.

She kissed him back, her body pressed against his, a low murmur of need whispering up from her throat and into his mouth.

His mind fuzzed, and his body blazed with more than mere

lust. More than desire or need…with a sense so primal he could almost hear the battle cries of his ancestors. That bellow echoed within his very cells.

Tangling his fingers in her thick hair, he tightened his hold and angled her face so he could go deeper. Pulling her tighter into him, he held her easily up and off the floor. He felt more powerful than gravity.

His other hand moved down her back and flanks to encircle her waist. She wrapped her legs around his hips.

Heat surrounded him, and he pushed his groin hard against hers. His cock pulsed in perfect agreement—get in and now.

"Yoo-hoo," a cheery voice chirped as the kitchen door opened.

Hawk dropped Dawn to her feet and whirled around, reaching for the knife he'd forgotten to place at his hip. His gun was on the nightstand. His heart thundered, and the room narrowed into sharp focus as he moved to defend.

"Hawk," Dawn hissed, shoving at his waist. "Relax." Her voice was low and throaty, and so sexy a shiver dashed down his torso. "It's Mrs. Hudson."

Hawk took in the scene, forcing his body to relax. "Hi, Mrs. H."

Mrs. Hudson, wearing a bright purple down jacket with "Hot Mama" bedazzled across the front, led Mrs. Poppins into the room.

Mrs. Poppins sighed. "Oh my."

Mrs. Hudson whacked Mrs. P. with a humongous purse. "Look what you did, Bernie. Just look what you did."

Hawk cleared his throat and fought the urge to shuffle his feet. Dawn stepped up next to him, her face a blazing scarlet.

Mrs. Hudson, oddly enough, looked more regretful than righteous or judgmental. "The cow, Dawnie. Come on. Surely you understood about the cow, sweetie."

Dawn swallowed audibly. "Yes, ma'am."

Hawk frowned, turning from Mrs. Hudson to Dawn to Mrs. Poppins. "Is there a problem with the herd, ladies?"

Mrs. Poppins coughed. "No, young man. It's more of a milk issue and making it too readily available."

Mrs. Hudson sighed. "Well, that's two down. There are still three rules we could employ. I mean, he didn't really rescue her last night, you know? You should've called him *before* she changed the tire." Then, catching herself up short, she peered through bright red glasses at Hawk. "Don't you have somewhere to be today, Hawk Rain?"

When she used that voice and gave him that look, he felt eight years old again. "Actually, I do." He had to get back to work, which meant he had to stop thinking about sweet Dawn Freeze and concentrate.

Dawn gave him a pleading "don't leave me" look, and he couldn't help a quick grin. Yeah. The darlin' was on her own. He turned toward her bedroom so he could fetch his clothing. "Dawn? I'd like to speak to you for a moment." He didn't wait to make sure she followed, knowing full well she'd want to escape the two biddies.

"We'll make you some coffee, dear," Mrs. Hudson piped up.

"Thanks," Dawn said weakly from behind him. Seconds later, she swished into the bedroom and shut the door quietly. "Oh my God. Seriously. Oh my God."

Hawk chuckled and yanked on his shirt. "What's going on with the Poppins' cows? I thought the dairy was doing well."

Dawn made a sound like a cross between a garbled drunk and a wet cat. "I'm not sure, but don't worry about it. I'm sure the ladies are way off base and just looking for some company."

Lie. Total, evasive lie. Interesting. Hawk narrowed his focus on her stoic face and cocked his head. He could push for an answer, but when it came to cows, he really didn't care. "If you need my help, you'll let me know, right?"

She coughed. "Ah, yeah. You've done enough already, believe me."

As much as he'd love to stick around to figure out the subtext of that statement, he now had a job to do. "When I said it was a mistake, I meant more in a timing aspect than anything else."

Her eyebrow rose. Totally a Lodge-Freeze move. "What does that mean?"

How much should he tell her? "We just need to pick this up in a month or so and not now."

"Why?" she asked.

"I can't tell you," he admitted. The less she knew about Meyer, the better. She'd let her family know, and then he'd have his best friends in danger. Or worse, she'd try to help him, and then he'd have to worry about her. She shouldn't be anywhere near a drug cartel. Plus, though he'd go to the grave before admitting it, he felt guilty Meyer was on the loose, as if he'd failed. He didn't want Dawn to know about that, even if she was supportive. "I'm sorry. You can't know."

"Bullshit." She lifted her chin in the way that all but provoked him to kiss her again. "Stop being an asshole."

He actually hated it when she swore. Odd, but true. Such a pretty mouth shouldn't say such things. "I'm done with that language, Dawnie."

She blinked, and her head went back. "Excuse me?"

"I know I swear, and I promise I won't do it around you any longer. I shouldn't have last night. But it isn't right coming from you," he said, feeling like a jackass.

She smiled. "Fuck you to hell and back, you fuckturd of a shithead misogynist bastard of a dickheaded idiot."

He couldn't help it. He threw back his head and laughed his ass off, temporarily releasing the tension gripping his guts. "If you were mine, you'd be over my knee right now." Which he'd love to see anyway.

She rolled her eyes. "Good thing I'm not yours, and if you ever tried it, I guarantee you'd lose a testicle."

That was Dawnie. She'd fight dirty and go right for the balls. "So long as we understand each other," he said dryly.

She glanced at the bed. "I don't understand the timing problem."

"Okay." He owed her the truth. "You're right, and my holding it a secret is more about pride than anything else. So here are the full facts, and I'm asking you to keep them to yourself. I don't need Colton on my six for this one, considering he has twins coming any day. My last mission involved putting away a real bastard, one who betrayed not only my unit but our country, and now he's escaped."

Dawn's gaze sharpened. "And?"

"I made a promise to my unit, as well as to Reese, that I'd put him away for good and destroy his entire organization. It looks like he's fled south, and I need to start tracking him before he completely disappears."

Her pretty face paled. "How dangerous is he?"

"He's a moron interested in money and nothing else. Right now, I assume, he's hiding under a rock," Hawk said.

"Sounds like a job for the police or DEA," she retorted.

Hawk nodded. "Yeah, I know. It's a military issue, and the military is after him, too. But the DOD is covering all its bases, so they've also contracted Reese's company. Right now, nobody cares who brings in Meyer, but I know it'd be a big deal for Reese to accomplish the job."

"What does any of this have to do with me?"

"Nothing, but I don't want you dealing with the gossips after I'm gone, and even though Meyer is a twit, he's involved in the drug trade, and who knows what his allies are like. The safest course for you, on so many fronts, is just to stay away from me for now," he said.

She swallowed. "No."

His head jerked back. "Excuse me?"

"I said no. No bad guy is going to dictate my life or keep you away from family and friends. Think, Hawk," she said.

He shook his head. "Think?"

"Yeah. Look at the backup you have here. Quinn and Jake were dangerous in the military, although I don't know the half of it. Colton is an MMA champion and can be mean as a bull if he wants. My dad was in the service and can fight and shoot. Frankly, testosterone isn't necessary to protect and defend. My mom and sisters-in-law all know how to grapple and shoot, as do I. Nobody messes with family. We're your people, and on the off chance you need backup, you have it," she said, meeting his gaze evenly.

What a sweetheart. If she hadn't owned his heart before, she sure did now. "Quinn, Jake, Colton, and your dad have families." And thus weaknesses. "You women are tough, but you have no clue what I'm dealing with. I can't involve any of you." Plus, this would take time, and he couldn't take them away from their kids. Not to mention that his particular brand of hunting was a specific skill set. No doubt the Lodge-Freeze men and women could hold their own, but they hadn't signed on with Reese's company, which specialized in tracking criminals. That was his job.

Sadness darkened her eyes. "That's your choice, Hawk. But I liked what we started here and don't really feel like putting us on hold. We can be discreet."

She didn't get it. The woman truly didn't understand, and part of him was thankful for that. To do what he needed to do, he couldn't be the guy holding her at night. He didn't even want her to suspect, much less glimpse, the man he had to become right now. "Sorry, baby. This is my way. Period."

"Fine." Her eyes blazed ten kinds of fire, chased by sorrow. "Do your thing. I may be here, I may not."

Oh, she'd be there. "Fair enough." He yanked on his boots

57

and strode toward the kitchen, where the elderly ladies were filling coffee cups. "Have a nice day, ladies."

Mrs. Hudson sighed. "We'll try. Peter, Paul, and Mary. There's so much more work to do now."

Mrs. Poppins nodded sagely.

Hawk frowned as he shoved open the door. Didn't matter if a woman was in her twenties or her seventies…he didn't understand a damn one of them.

For now, it was time to hunt.

CHAPTER 7

Women need to stick together... for sanity if not for survival. ~ The Lady Elks Secret Archives.

A FULL DAY and night after Hawk had blown her world apart, Dawn played with the plastic lid on her coffee. She'd ordered the double latte to go from Kurt's Koffees but had quickly been intercepted by her sister-in-law, Juliet. Dawn smiled at the gorgeous redhead and straightened in her seat. Juliet was the classiest and most graceful woman Dawn had ever met, and a secret part of her wished to be that smooth. Juliet had married Dawn's older brother, Quinn, and continued to run a successful western art gallery in town.

The round plastic tables were about half filled with folks wearing snow boots and heavy jackets. Painted snowmen and dancing Santas decorated the wide windows, and Christmas music played in the background.

Juliet smiled. "What's wrong, Dawnie?"

"I slept with Hawk." The words came out before she could stop them, before she could think twice.

Juliet's eyebrows arched in a truly classic face. "Oh my goodness."

Yeah. That about summed it up. "I shouldn't have said anything, I know," Dawn rushed on. Juliet owed her loyalty to Quinn. They'd only been married a short time, and Dawn's older brother would not be happy about such news. In fact, his head would probably implode, and he'd reach for his gun. "I'm so sorry."

"Why?" Juliet sipped her mocha. "You need to talk, right?"

Yeah. Definitely. But she'd figured she'd talk to Melanie, whom she'd known for, well, ever. "Yes, but I don't mean to put you in a difficult position."

Julie chuckled. "I don't have to tell your brother everything, you know. You and I also have a relationship, and I always wanted a sister so badly. Now I have you, Sophie, and Melanie, and we women have to stick together around here."

So freakin' true. "The sex was amazing." Dawn frowned and focused on her coffee cup.

"Why do you look like somebody kicked your puppy?" Juliet asked softly.

The door chimed, and a vivacious blonde popped inside and hustled their way. "Man, it's cold out there," Sophie Lodge chirped, dropping into the seat next to Juliet. She'd married Dawn's oldest brother, Jake, and already had three kids with him. "What's going on, ladies? You look like you're solving the world's problems over coffee."

Dawn gulped. "Hawk and I almost broke my headboard last night."

Sophie stilled. Her eyes opened wide, as did her mouth. Her lips smacked together and pure, unadulterated glee lit her small features. "It's about time." She chuckled. "Man, your brothers are going to blow a gasket." She squinted toward Juliet. "Is Quinn up-to-date on his life insurance? I can see his head exploding off his shoulders."

"That's what I said," Dawn muttered.

Juliet cleared her throat. "Good point. What about Jake?"

Sophie shrugged. "Jake will shoot first and freak later. He's a great lawyer and can probably get himself off with an insanity charge. Quinn's the sheriff and can't shoot first." Amusement glimmered in her eyes. "Although I assume we're not telling the guys? That Dawn and Hawk want some privacy to figure things out?"

Juliet smiled. "I believe that's the plan."

Dawn cleared her throat. "I'm sitting right here, you two. Knock it off."

Sophie clapped her gloved hands together. "Sorry, but this it too great not to have fun." Then she frowned. "Why aren't you doing the *happy I got laid* dance? I mean, it's Hawk. *Hawk.*" She gasped and sat back in her chair. "Oh no. Did Hawk suck in bed?"

Dawn slapped her palm against her forehead. What had she been thinking to talk about Hawk to her sisters-in-law? They were both crazy. Sure, Juliet masked it better, but a fireball lurked behind her classy exterior. Sophie didn't even hide the nuttiness. "Hawk was a god in bed."

Sophie leaned forward and patted the table. "So you, ah, you know?"

For the love of Pete. "Yes. I *you knowed* four times," Dawn admitted.

Juliet's eyebrows rose. "Four times? Very nice."

Dawn pinched the bridge of her nose. Heat rushed through her head. "Then in the morning, Hawk got a phone call from Reese, and some bad guy he put away has escaped, so we need to keep our distance until he takes care of it. All by himself."

Sophie snorted. "Moron."

Juliet nodded. "Idiot."

"Exactly." Dawn swept her hands out wide. "How dumb is that?"

Juliet's eyes narrowed. "Tell me you kept your cool. Played it very nonchalant."

Dawn smiled, and it even felt mean. "Oh yeah. I told him he didn't need to be alone, but if that was his choice, not to let the door hit his ass."

"Perfect," Sophie said.

Juliet drew out her cell phone and punched in a number.

Dawn shook her head. "What are you doing?"

Juliet held up a hand. "Reese? Hi. It's Juliet Lodge. What is going on with Hawk?"

Dawn sat back, going still as Juliet tapped her fingers on the table.

"Well, I suggest you get your behind in gear and take care of the problem. You should probably call the Lodge-Freeze guys before they find out, from, well, me." Juliet smiled, her voice cultured, her gaze street mean. "We do look forward to seeing you." She disengaged the call.

Dawn gaped. "What did you just do?"

Juliet lifted a slim shoulder. "We've kept in touch since the whole kidnapping issue." A drug runner had kidnapped Juliet when Reese still worked for the DEA, and he'd helped in her rescue. She turned to Sophie and wiggled her eyebrows. "He's coming to town."

Dawn smiled. "Excellent. It'd be nice to have Reese here."

"Yes, it would. He should move here and find something less dangerous to do," Sophie said.

The door jangled and Melanie waddled in, crossed the room, and took the seat next to Dawn with a deep sigh. "I'm huge."

Juliet reached over and brushed snow from Mel's shoulder. "You're perfect."

Mel snorted. "Right. What's up?"

Sophie leaned forward. "Dawn and Hawk did the nasty, they're not telling anybody, Hawk has to go chase a drug dealer, and Reese is coming to town."

Melanie blinked. She slowly turned toward Dawn and lowered her chin, her eyes wide. "You and Hawk?"

Dawn's stomach turned over. "Um, yeah." She rubbed her hands together. Melanie, Colton, and Hawk had been best friends forever, and Mel had always been protective of both men. When she and Colton had finally gotten together, they'd made sure to keep Hawk close. Asking Melanie to keep the secret from Colton wasn't fair. Dawn sighed. "I know it's unexpected." How mad was Mel going to get?

Melanie leaned forward. "How is Hawk in bed? I've always wondered."

Sophie snorted out a laugh.

Mel rolled her eyes. "Just out of curiosity. I've always loved Colton, but I've heard so many rumors about Hawk. Are they true?"

Dawn's body relaxed, and she smiled. "They're true."

"I knew it." Melanie smacked the table. Her smile faded. "Oh. I'm not supposed to tell Colton."

"No," Juliet said.

Dawn fidgeted on her chair. "I know it's not fair to ask you to keep a secret."

Melanie rubbed her protruding belly. "I'm pregnant. Don't worry—I can get away with anything right now. By the way, the doctor heard two heartbeats yesterday, and everything is just fine."

Dawn smiled. Melanie hadn't thought she'd be able to have kids, and to be having twins was more than the woman had ever dreamed about. "Of course you're all fine. Colton with twins—I love it."

Even though she was beyond happy for Melanie, her mind kept going back to her love life. What was she going to do about Hawk?

The door jangled again, and Mrs. Hudson trooped inside with Mrs. Poppins, heading right toward her. Henry Bullton, after holding open the door, hitched up his gray pants and strutted to the counter. The scent of Irish Spring and Ben Gay wafted in his wake.

"Dawn Eleanor Freeze," Mrs. Hudson said, drawing herself up to her full five-foot height, sparkles dancing across her chest. "We really must talk."

Sophie jumped to her feet. "I require coffee." She leaned down and assisted Melanie up. "You need tea."

Juliet slid gracefully from the table. "I'll be powdering my nose."

Dawn barely kept from glaring as her sisters-in-law all deserted her like rats fleeing a sinking ship. She sighed instead. "Mrs. Hudson, Mrs. Poppins. How lovely to see you. Please have a seat."

* * *

ON HIS OWN PROPERTY, with the morning light illuminating the snowy mountains around him, Hawk snipped off a piece of barbed wire, his hat shielding his face from the burning wind. Snow covered the fields, and in the distance, trees dumped more of the powder as the storm assailed them. "How are the northern pastures?"

Colton glanced over after resetting a downed fence post. He'd pulled his hat low and his coat high to combat the wind, while heavy leather gloves protected his hands. "Quinn and Jake just finished repairs from the last storm and wanted to meet in town for breakfast."

Hawk swallowed and bent to his task, his gut churning. He'd been working since first light with Colton, on the fences separating their properties, and guilt about Dawn ate through him like termites. No way could he sit at breakfast with all three of her older brothers and not confess everything. Especially since Reese would hit town again soon, and Hawk would leave. He should never have slept with Dawn knowing he was going to be leaving in less than a week.

But the woman was a grown-up, and she deserved her privacy.

He probably should've called her the previous day or night, but he hadn't known what to say. A part of him, a small part he didn't like, was peeved she hadn't called him. "I think I'll just check the other side of my property and meet up with y'all later."

"We checked those the day before you came home. Jake and I did," Colton said absently, kicking the post and making sure it stayed in place.

Well, of course they had. That's what family did.

Colton stretched his back. "I thought you and I could head by the gyms and check them out. They're going well, and we're offering a couple of free self-defense classes that I need help with. Could you take over instructing a couple while you're home?"

"I'm probably leaving too soon, but when I get back, I will." Dang it. He was part owner and should step up and work. "Sorry I haven't been around."

"You're here now." Colton tossed some pliers in the back of the work truck.

Hawk glanced at the snow-covered pastures, solid fences, and shockingly white mountains around them. The breeze cut into him with the scents of pine and snow, and the tension in his chest lessened. "I'm here now," he repeated. Yeah. Home. Finally. He shoved his hat back on his head. "Colt? We gotta talk."

Colton turned, blue eyes lasering through him. "I figured. I think it's time you retired from whatever you've been doing and stayed home."

"I made a promise for one more job, and I have to keep that promise." Not only that, taking down Meyer meant dismantling the entire organization, and that might take Hawk years.

A rumble came down the lane, and snow spit in every direction. A black work truck came into view, rolling to a stop near theirs. Quinn jumped from the driver's side, and Jake from the passenger's.

Hawk nodded at what amounted to older brothers for him. Quinn had taught him to fight, and Jake had taught him to shoot. Both skills had saved his ass more than once in the military. They had their father's size and their mother's Native American features, leaving them long, lean, and sometimes mean, with black hair and even darker eyes. Their dad had died in a snowmobile accident, and their mom had later married Tom Freeze before having Colt and Dawn. They weren't Tom Freeze's biological kids, but they moved like him, all grace and muscle.

Quinn smiled and grabbed him in a solid hug. "Welcome home."

Hawk smacked Quinn on the back. "Sheriff."

Jake was next, his eyes dark, his jeans ripped. "Glad you're safe."

He returned the hug and then backed away. "Thought we were meeting for breakfast."

Quinn leaned against the truck, his black cowboy hat gathering slowly falling snow. "Figured we'd talk now."

Hawk braced his legs. If they hit him, he'd take it, and he wouldn't hit back. He deserved the punch. "Okay."

Colton stilled. "What are we talking about?"

Jake rubbed his whiskered chin. "Reese called us and told us everything about your current mission."

Heat exploded up Hawk's throat. "Son of a bitch."

Quinn's gaze hardened. "We should've heard it from you and not from Reese."

Yeah, maybe. "This is my problem, and you all have families

to worry about," Hawk said.

Colton glanced from his older brothers to Hawk. "What is there to worry about?"

Hawk blinked, belatedly realizing they didn't know about him and Dawn. He should probably say something. "I hunted and captured a drug distributor who had been an acquaintance of mine in the military, and he apparently has escaped and needs to be found."

Colton shoved his hat all the way back. "I knew you were working for Reese, but why didn't you tell me about this?" Anger rode the words hard, and his shoulders went large and stiff beneath his coat.

Hawk met his best friend's anger head on. "You're newly married, and you have twins on the way. The last thing you have time for is chasing a drug dealer across the world with me. Besides, it could be dangerous."

Jake shook his head. "You're a dumb sonuvabitch."

Quinn nodded, while Colton still hadn't moved.

"I'm sorry." Hawk sidled away from the barbed wire and closer to the truck. If he got hit, he'd rather plow into steel than sharp wire. "This is my problem, one I thought I'd solved before heading home, but I guess I was wrong. I thought the dangerous part of my job was over, but I'm going to have to go back to it."

"You're family, you idiot," Colton growled.

Yeah, Hawk was family. He needed to change that, at least for a while, in order to keep them safe. There was only one thing he could say to get them to back off and leave him alone. He didn't want to do it, but to protect them, to protect everybody, he'd take the beating. So he planted his boots in the snow. "I slept with Dawn the night before last."

Silence roared in on a tension that took up all the oxygen. Even the wind quieted.

Colton somehow moved to intercept Quinn, but Jake was

still the fastest guy around. His fist connected with Hawk's jaw before Hawk could blink.

Lightning exploded through his head, and he started to go down.

Quinn caught him before he hit the snow. "Jesus. Did you have to hit him so hard?"

"Yes," Jake growled. Then he leaned in, his breath heating the stars swirling across Hawk's vision. "You okay, Hawk?"

"Uh." Hawk regained his feet and shook his head, wincing as pain lanced behind his eyes. "I'm okay."

Jake clapped him on the back and held tight until he regained his balance. "I should've pulled the punch more."

More? "I'm fine." Hawk squinted, relieved when he could see again. "So I guess this is it."

Jake frowned. "This is what?" He winced. "Do you think I gave him a concussion?"

Quinn grabbed Hawk's lapels and jerked him around, studying his eyes. "His pupils are okay."

Hawk shoved him off and shook his head again. "Jesus. I'm fine."

Colton ducked his head to study Hawk's jaw. "Man, mom is going to be pissed, Jake."

Jake grimaced. "Ugh."

Hawk tried to grasp the conversation, but his ears still rang a little. "I know, and I'm sorry. I'll apologize to Loni."

Colton frowned. "Maybe he *is* concussed."

"I'm fine," Hawk snapped.

Colton snorted. "Mom will be pissed Jake hit you. He's the one who's going to be in the doghouse."

Hawk tried to keep his stance normal. "She'll be mad at me."

"Nah." Quinn clapped his arm around Hawk's shoulders. "She'll be thrilled. Let's go grab breakfast, and we can figure out what to do about this guy you're chasing, as well as the other part of your dumb-ass plan to finish off his organization all by yourself."

Hawk tried to shake his head again. "No." This was all wrong. "You guys are supposed to be pissed."

Quinn shrugged and nearly knocked Hawk over. "You got hit, it's done. You're family, Hawk. Nothing changes that."

Emotion, unexpected and unwelcome, detonated in Hawk's chest. Family. His eyes teared. "Maybe I am concussed."

CHAPTER 8

Good food fills a man's stomach, warms his brain, and sends him jewelry shopping. ~The Lady Elks Secret Archives

DAWN FINISHED GLAZING the chicken breast in her cheery kitchen, muttering to herself the entire time. A fire crackled in the big stone fireplace, and snow piled against the windowsill. Hawk hadn't called. After what had been the most amazing night of her life, the bastard hadn't called in two days.

So he had meant it that they needed to keep their distance.

What an idiot.

She'd even had trouble sleeping without him.

An entire day at the office crunching numbers hadn't helped any. Colton had been absent all day, so she'd spent some time talking to Anne and just working.

Now she ate alone. Again.

A rap on the door caught her up short. She wiped her hands on a towel and hurried to open it.

Hawk stood on the porch, a bottle of Shiraz in his hand. "Hi."

She stepped back. Her hair was piled haphazardly on her

head, she wore no makeup, and her yoga pants had a rip across one knee. "What are you doing here?"

He lifted a shoulder and stepped closer. "I thought we should talk." A dark bruise marred the left side of his chiseled jaw.

"What happened to your face?" she asked, her heart sinking.

"Let me in," he said.

She paused. In faded jeans and a black jacket, with his dark hair pulled back and his even darker green eyes glimmering with a light she couldn't quite identify, Hawk was every possible definition of a smart girl's *oh hell no*. She stood aside. "Come on in."

He brushed by her, surrounding her with the scent of snow and male.

She closed the door. "I'm making chicken." If any of her friends just showed up, she'd feed them, so why not Hawk?

"Sounds good. Mel made steak last night." He shrugged out of his jacket to hang it on a hook by the door. "I'd forgotten how good home-cooked food tasted."

The edge she'd always sensed in Hawk had sharpened, focused with a palpable tension since the phone call from Reese. For the first time in her life, she could actually see the deadly soldier he'd become. How surprising he'd been able to hide that side of himself so well through the years.

Apparently he was done hiding. They'd seen each other naked, it had been fantastic, and now she didn't know what to say. She casually smoothed back her hair and headed toward the kitchen. "Open the wine and have a seat." Keeping her back to him, she tossed another couple of chicken breasts into the pan and smothered them with more of Mrs. Hudson's chicken glaze. Dawn had stocked up during the Fourth of July Fair.

Hawk worked smoothly beside her, uncorking the wine and pouring two glasses. "Come sit down." He handed her a glass and trucked the few steps to the living room.

Dawn swirled the wine and frowned. "When did you get so bossy?"

He shrugged. "Sorry."

The guy didn't sound sorry. She cleared her throat, her hand trembling around the glass. "This is weird." Without meeting his eyes, she crossed into the room and sat on the sofa. He sat next to her, and her breath quickened. Her nipples hardened, just from his heat, and darn it, she wished she'd worn a bra.

"I told your brothers about us sleeping together." Hawk placed his glass on the coffee table.

Fury rippled through her. "You what?" she yelled.

He calmly recaptured her wineglass, put it safely on the table, and turned to face her—serious eyes, bruised face, indomitable body. "I told them the truth."

"You moron," she said slowly.

He grinned, flashing a dimple.

Her gaze dropped to his jaw. "Which one of them hit you?"

"Jake."

Yeah, that made sense. She squinted. It was a heck of a bruise. "What happened then?"

"We ate breakfast and I explained about the case I've been on, the entire story." Hawk reached out to cup her chin. "I'm sorry I told them about us when I said I wouldn't, but we were all there, and I couldn't lie."

Something in the statement didn't make sense. "Baloney. You could lie." What in the world had he been thinking? Her mind rapidly clicked facts into place. "You wanted them mad." No way. Man, he was clueless sometimes. "You thought they'd turn their backs on you and let you deal with Meyer on your own."

"Yes," he admitted.

She scoffed. "You're so dumb."

His gaze warmed. "Apparently I miscalculated."

She exhaled, and her face heated. "If one of them, and I mean just one of them, tries to give me a safe sex talk, I'm kicking you so hard in the balls they'll fill your throat."

His smile widened. "I hope all three of them give you the safe sex talk. Man, I'd love to watch that."

She shook her head. "So much for privacy." Like there was any such thing in Maverick County. "Do my parents know?" Even an independent, grown-ass woman didn't want her dad knowing about her sex life.

"I doubt it." Hawk's thumb ran across her bottom lip.

Heat flared from his touch, zinged around her torso, and landed squarely between her legs. "Uh, well, what happens now?" Her mind had pretty much blanked.

His lids lowered to half-mast. "Your brothers and I are coming up with a plan for Meyer, and after tonight, you and I should keep our distance until we catch him. Just in case there's any fall out, which is unlikely."

She blinked, disbelief shooting through her. "My brothers and you came up with a plan."

"Yep," he said.

She sighed, wanting nothing more than to argue. "Like I said, you're an idiot."

"Meyer is a moron, but he's in bed with some pretty dangerous people. While I don't think any of them know about me, or more specifically where I'm from, I don't want to take a chance." An intensity, one fraught with concern, overtook the atmosphere, a tension emanating directly from Hawk. "Trust me, Dawnie."

"I can take care of myself." She was done being the overprotected little sister of the Lodge-Freeze clan.

Hawk nodded. "I know, but you have no idea how to deal with somebody like Meyer or his cohorts. Thank God."

She shook her head, more than a little slice of hurt piercing her chest. "You see me as incapable as my brothers do. As a kid."

Hawk's eyebrows rose. "Believe me, I see you as all grown up." His gaze dropped to her lips. "All woman."

His husky tone of voice licked right across her skin, and she shivered. "You know I'm not gonna wait for you, right? I'm not playing the helpless girl hiding behind a bunch of tough boys, now or in the future, if you decide to go off hunting again."

Hawk slid a hand through her hair and twisted at the nape. "Tough doesn't come close to what I'll be to protect you." His gaze didn't falter from her mouth. "You don't have to hide, but if you think any one of us will let you deal with drug runners, you're crazy." He leaned in and brushed his mouth across hers. "I'm not asking you to wait for me."

He wasn't, now was he? That should hurt, but instead, fire lit through her. Passion and anger boiled in her blood, heating her veins. They might not have forever, not if he didn't see the real her, but she'd take another night. One more to remember forever. Her tongue flicked out and slid along his lower lip.

He sucked in a breath.

Yeah. She smiled and did it again.

His eyelids lifted, and his gaze met hers. "You sure?"

"The chicken will take an hour." Just the thought of what Hawk could do with an hour softened her thighs. Oh, he didn't see her strength any more than her brothers did, that was for sure. But she'd wondered for so long, and the other night had been amazing. Part of her wanted to prove herself, to show him she was just as strong as her brothers, while the other part wanted to smack him in the head for being obtuse. He clamped a hand on her leg, and her body took over.

He smiled then, flashing smooth teeth in a warrior's face. Promise and warning hinted on his expression.

The promise she wanted, the warning she needed. A wildness lived in him, one similar to the thrum of her blood. For years she'd wondered if he could match her. Their people lived in houses and tamed the land around them, but every once in a while, she could hear the distant drums of her ancestors. Primitive and untamed. Somehow, she knew Hawk felt it too.

He turned, all casual muscle, and she ended up beneath him on the sofa. His hard body pressed her down, and his hands tunneled through her hair, loosening the tie. "I should've called last night," he rumbled, his lips above hers.

"Yeah. You should have." She widened her thighs and lifted her knees. They tipped on the edge of the couch. "You're too big for the couch."

He grinned, and the world spun. She landed on him on the carpet, and then he rolled them over, once again stretched out on top of her. The thick rug cushioned her back, while the fire crackled over them. "Better?" he asked.

Definitely. Hawk Rain above her, groin to groin, his chest lightly on hers? Perfect. Definitely perfect. "This will do," she murmured, wiggling her butt to get more comfortable.

"Glad to hear it." Another smooth movement, and he'd forced her shirt over her head.

She gasped, her insides quivering.

"No bra," he whispered, leaning down and licking a path between her breasts. Desire heated her, and she rubbed against him. He grinned, lifting up. "I bet you're ready for me."

Man, he was beautiful. Darker than danger green eyes, hard face, pure lethal man. "I was ready for you five years ago," she said.

The words changed him. Not in an obvious way, but in a moment as he paused and studied her. He shifted, fast and strong, and her yoga pants flew across the room. She jerked his shirt over his head, revealing hard muscle. Their movements became frantic as he shoved down his jeans and rolled on a condom with definite finesse.

He caressed down her torso and over her abdomen, sliding one finger across her clit.

Sparks shot through her.

He gently touched her, and she could feel her own wetness coating her thighs. "You're ready," he murmured.

Oh yeah, she was ready.

With one hard push, he buried himself to the hilt in her.

Pain and pleasure drove through her, and she threw back her head, arching her back. Too much. There was so much to Hawk. She breathed out, relaxing her body, trying to accept him.

His face was suddenly right above hers, his gaze intent, possession glimmering in his dark eyes. "Wet and ready, Dawn. Like I said."

She blinked, trying to focus, overcome by so much sensation her brain misfired. Skin to skin, Hawk was better than she'd ever imagined. "I'd say you're ready, too," she breathed, her body overcome.

His smile was all the more potent for its slowness. "Now would be a good time to talk."

His dick pulsed inside her, and his heated body trapped her. Her sex clenched round him, and a desperate urge to move tingled through her nerves. "Talk later," she moaned.

"Now," he said.

She tried to gyrate against him, and he grabbed her butt with one strong hand, holding her still. The other tangled in her hair and twisted, holding her easily in place. Her body trembled head to toe at the dominance, and the craving for him intensified. "Damn it, Hawk."

He kept her gaze, his eyes right above hers. "You're wrong that I don't see you, Dawn. That I think you're weak or anything less than you are."

Her mouth gaped, and she stilled. "Then what's the problem?"

"You're not seeing me. Not really," he said.

She frowned, her nerves firing. "I see you."

"No. I was a sniper and a hunter in the military. You've never seen that side of me, and I want to keep it that way. Just trust me to deal with the problem, and then we'll figure out us." He slid out and back in.

"Oh." She couldn't keep a low moan from escaping. "You're not alone."

"I know." His fingers tightened on her butt, and he started to fuck. No other word for it. Hard and fast, he drove into her, hammering with impressive strength.

Helpless in his hold, all she could do was feel. The first orgasm rushed over her, making her cry out, building again within seconds of completion. He surged deeper, holding tight, and tension rose inside her, until she couldn't breathe. "Hawk," she whispered.

"There it is." He angled up, hitting her clit, and she roared into an orgasm.

The room flashed white and hot and her body convulsed as she came. The second she relaxed with a soft sigh, Hawk shoved inside and held still, jerking with his release.

The fire crackled around them as they panted against each other. Dawn's heart raced, and she took deep breaths to calm down. He nipped her lip and grinned. "Absolutely beautiful."

She warmed and smiled. Hawk Rain thought she was beautiful.

He slid out of her and stretched to stand, pulling her up with him by the biceps. "Be right back." Turning, all sleek muscle, he headed toward the bathroom, no doubt to get rid of the condom.

Her knees wobbled. Swallowing several times, she yanked on her shirt and searched for her yoga pants. She spotted them on the kitchen counter. Grinning, she crossed the room and pulled them on. Grasping potholders, she took the chicken from the stove and dished up two plates.

Hawk returned, fully nude. "We're not eating naked?"

Her mouth went dry. "Um."

He chuckled and grabbed his jeans from the floor, tugging

them up and leaving the top unbuttoned. "Smells amazing, Dawnie." He quickly secured the wineglasses and sat at the table. "Man, I've missed food."

She took her seat, suddenly shy.

Hawk dug in. "Phenomenal," he muttered, reaching for his wine. "Is there anything you can't do?"

Her head lifted, and she smiled. "Anybody can cook chicken."

"Right." He took another big bite, eating happily.

She took a bite. It really was good. Mrs. Hudson's glazes were known throughout Montana for their deliciousness. Something tickled in the back of Dawn's brain, but she shook it off.

Hawk took a drink of wine and then coughed. He coughed again.

Dawn frowned. "You okay?"

"Yeah." Hawk turned to the side and coughed harder.

Dawn jumped up and poured him a glass of water. "Hawk?"

He took the water and downed the entire glass. "I'm fine, Dawnie."

Then he coughed again, his eyes widening.

Oh no, oh no. Dawn grabbed the glaze to read the neatly typed ingredients. She hadn't thought. "Strawberries." She whirled around toward Hawk, who has holding his throat. "I didn't think. When I bought it, you'd already left town. I didn't think." She scrambled for the phone. Hawk had had an allergy to strawberries his whole life. "EpiPen?"

He shook his head, his mouth gaping open.

"Oh God." She quickly dialed 911 as Hawk pitched forward and onto the floor.

CHAPTER 9

There's strength and power in softness. ~ The Lady Elks Secret Archives.

A BOMB FLASHED *white and hot across Hawk's vision. He ducked, recoiling from the burning fire. Cries of pain echoed in his mind.*

The dream morphed to the day he discovered his friend, his fellow soldier, had been funneling drugs.

"What have you been thinking?" he asked Meyer, standing with their buddy, Chancy Plet, a very tough soldier from Colorado, who was as furious as Hawk.

Meyer stood in the desert night, ignoring the wind throwing sand around them. Brown hair, buzz cut, and serious dark eyes. "I'm tired of the bullshit, Hawk. The drugs are getting in with or without us, and we can do more good with the money than anybody else. Don't you think?"

Hawk shook his head. They'd fought together for three months, which in the desert, was a lifetime. "This isn't you." Sure, Meyer had jumped into danger more than once, often recklessly, but war was war.

They all had to be crazy to survive it. "Tell me you haven't gone too far."

Meyer shrugged. "Define 'too far.' I've moved drugs, made deals, and done my time."

No. Done his time? He'd killed for the drug business—for greed. Even so, Hawk tried to save him. "Let me help you get out of this. We'll turn you in, say it was a mistake, and figure out what do now."

Meyer nodded. "Fine." Then he pivoted, just enough, and stabbed Chancy in the gut.

The world slowed to a stop. Hawk reacted, lunging forward and taking Meyer to the ground. Pain ripped through his thigh, and he glanced down to yank the blade out, punching at the same time.

Meyer jumped up and ran.

Hawk, bleeding profusely, turned to his injured friend on the ground. He'd be all right, but it took time to recuperate from gut wounds, unfortunately. "I'll get him. I promise you, he'll spend eternity in prison for this."

Hawk woke from the nightmare and sat up, reaching for the knife not strapped to his hip.

"You're okay," said a rough voice from his left.

Hawk fought a chill from the cool air. The smell of bleach filled his nostrils. He turned to find Quinn Lodge kicked back in a hospital guest chair, gun at his leg, badge at his belt, and a plastic cup of pudding in one broad hand. Hawk glanced down at his gown and tracked the ticking of the machine next to the bed. He yanked the oxygen tubes from his nose. "Is that my pudding?" he croaked.

Quinn swallowed a spoonful. "Yep. Vanilla, and it's really good. You want some?"

Hawk's stomach rolled. "No." He fell back against the pillows. "Is Dawn okay?"

"She's fine." Quinn placed the empty container on the bright orange counter. "A bit panicked, but I got to you before the ambulance and had an EpiPen on hand. Why didn't you?"

Hawk scrubbed both hands down his still swollen face. "Just got home and hadn't stocked up." He grimaced. "I dropped in on Dawn unexpectedly, and I'm sure she wasn't thinking about strawberries. This is my fault." His throat felt like he'd swallowed a combination of torn sandpaper and broken Christmas ornaments. "Sorry."

"No worries. It happens." Quinn's dark eyes darkened further. "That was quite a nightmare you were having."

Hawk took a deep breath. "I'm fine, Quinn."

"I know. Want to talk about it?"

"Sure. Meyer stabbed me and my friend. I promised to catch his ass and shut him down. Apparently I'm failing," Hawk snapped.

Quinn adjusted the badge at his belt. "Your friend okay?"

"Yeah, now. But it took some serious hospital and rehab time." In fact, Chancy was safely in Idaho running a bed and breakfast with a woman he'd known forever.

Quinn swallowed. "Have you seen anybody? For the nightmares, I mean?" The sheriff was like a bloodhound with a scent when he wanted answers.

"Yes." Hawk picked at the tape for the IV stuck in his elbow. "I've seen somebody, and still do via Skype once in a while." He wasn't stupid enough to think he could beat PTSD all on his own. "It's better."

Quinn nodded. "We have a group that meets the first Thursday of every month, if you want to join. I mean, once you finish with Meyer and whatever the rest of the dumb-ass mission is."

Hawk lifted an eyebrow. "I thought you all met to play poker."

Quinn shrugged. "We play poker, and sometimes we talk if somebody needs to talk to others who've been there. If nobody needs to talk, we drink and take all of Jake's money. He sucks at poker."

Jake had served two tours and bore the scars well. He was also one of the best lawyers in the Pacific Northwest and could bluff with the best of them. "I somehow doubt that," Hawk muttered.

Quinn rested his hand on his badge. "This reminds me of not too long ago when you were in the hospital. You said you were in a helicopter wreck, but in truth had been in quite the fight."

Hawk stilled.

Quinn cleared his throat. "It occurred to me, somewhat belatedly, I admit, that perhaps this Meyer you told us about had something to do with your condition."

Hawk met his friend's gaze levelly. "Even if I was no longer in the military, I was under orders, and I took a job. I've told you everything." He'd had a brutal fight on his hands when he'd taken on Meyer's men, and he'd won, although Meyer had not been present. Which was why Hawk had hunted him down after Colton's marriage. Now he had to do it all over again.

Quinn studied him, no expression crossing his hard face. "You just told me the rest of it."

The door opened, and a bundle of pure energy careened into the room and leaped for the bed. "Uncle Hawk."

Hawk grinned and scooted over for Leila Lodge to scamper up the bed and pat his face. The girl was Jake and Sophie's oldest kid and only daughter. So far. "Hey, sweetheart."

She clucked her tongue and shook her head. "Your face is huge. It looks like a blowfish without the blue color."

Hawk studied the girl, suddenly regretting his time away. She was growing so fast and would soon celebrate her ninth birthday. Her dark hair was twisted in braids that enhanced her delicate bone structure and stunning dark eyes, her heritage evident in every fragile line. "How'd you get here?"

"Great-grandpapa brought me."

He straightened. "Chief Lodge?" The chief of the Kooskia

Tribe had been on an extended tropical cruise for a month, and Hawk hadn't realized he'd returned home.

"Yep." Leila patted his cheeks again. "But he had to go to a meeting and said to tell you to get better and not be mad at Dawn. Uncle Quinn is supposed to take me home."

Hawk smiled. "I'm not mad at Dawn."

Leila leaned forward, her small lips pursing. "Are you sure? Great-Grandpapa said Dawn tried to poison you because you're, ah, a numb nuts."

Hawk coughed out, "Excuse me?"

Leila nodded, braids swinging. "Yep. He said that you've sat on your hands long enough and it's about time Dawn did something to get your attention. Even if it did almost kill you."

Hawk glanced over to find Quinn's face red, his body visibly struggling to keep from erupting in laughter. "I think the poisoning was an accident, sweetheart," Hawk said slowly, cutting a hard look at his friend.

Leila snorted. "I know. Aunt Dawn wouldn't try to hurt you on purpose. Though are you done sitting on your hands?"

Hawk sputtered out a non-answer, hoping Quinn would intercede. "Quinn?"

The sheriff leaned forward and tugged on one of Leila's braids. "Well? I'm with Leila and the chief. Have you stopped sitting on your hands?"

* * *

DAWN SAT in the empty hospital waiting room, her head back against the wall, her eyes closed. The plastic chairs were about a hundred years old and scratched her legs, even through her jeans. Christmas music played from the speakers, and the too-strong scent of disinfectant almost burned her nostrils. Quinn had been joking when he'd said he wanted to take Hawk's statement, right? Nobody in his right mind would think she'd tried to harm Hawk on purpose.

"Oh my, oh my, oh my," a voice twittered, coming closer.

Dawn opened her eyes to see Mrs. Hudson beelining toward her with a limping Mrs. Poppins on her heels.

"You tried to kill him," Mrs. Hudson said, dropping her bird-like frame into the adjacent seat as she removed a plastic head cover from her hair. "What now?"

Mrs. Poppins, in bright purple snow boots, remained standing, favoring one foot and wringing her bony hands together. "What now? She's broken rule number three. More importantly, we can't get her a man if she's in prison." She took the chair on the other side of Dawn, her lilac perfume soothing. "Oh, sweetie. Killing them is never the answer." She pursed her lips. "Well, it's *almost* never the answer."

Mrs. Hudson patted a startling spiral of sparkles down her bright blue pants. Even her green ski-jacket had yellow stones decorating the collar. "Listen. We can provide an alibi, right? If you have an alibi, they can't send you to prison."

Mrs. Poppins shook her head. "Alibi? Like what?"

"I'll take the rap. Say I traded the glaze for one with strawberries." Mrs. Hudson's wobbly chin firmed, and she sniffed. "Yes. That's what we'll say."

Mrs. Poppins leaned around Dawn. "Why would you do that? I mean, you need a motive, right?"

Mrs. Hudson bit her lip. "Yes. Lust. Unrequited lust. I've wanted Hawk Rain"—she wrinkled her nose and coughed delicately—"in my bed for years. He's quite, ah, um, sexy?"

Dawn dropped her chin to her chest. This wasn't happening. "I appreciate the help, ladies, but I'm pretty sure Hawk won't press charges." Unless he thought she'd poisoned him on purpose because of his stubbornness. "Mrs. Poppins? Why are you limping?"

"Ah, well, dear. I'm limping because I was helping Patty here stalk sweet Hawk. I fell on ice in his driveway trying to see into his window."

Dawn lifted an eyelid and glanced to the side. "You did not."

Mrs. Poppins shifted on the chair, color filtering through the papery skin on her face. "Well, we weren't checking out his place because of, you know, the lust. We were just dropping by to have a nice chat with him and take him some cookies baked by you, and I slipped on the walk."

Dawn sat up, her stomach twisting. "Are you all right?"

"Fine." She sniffed. "Turned out you had just poisoned him. We heard the call come over the police scanner in Patty's car once we discovered Hawk wasn't home."

Dawn sighed. "I thought Quinn confiscated that scanner."

Mrs. Hudson shook her head. "He did, but he didn't have a legal reason to do so, and my lawyer told him exactly that."

Dawn bit back a grin. "Was Jake your lawyer?"

"Of course, sweetie. Jake is everyone's lawyer." Mrs. Hudson patted Dawn's hand. "It was quite enjoyable seeing your brothers go toe-to-toe for a moment, but Jake had to do his job since I hired him, and Quinn had to listen because he's a good sheriff."

Dawn rubbed her nose. "Did you mention cookies?"

"I baked them and was gonna tell Hawk you did." Mrs. Hudson shook her head, her lips turned down. "Now you've broken three rules. Please tell me you're not still giving it away."

Dawn sputtered, her face heating.

"Oh good Lord," Mrs. Poppins twittered. "Stop having the sex with that man." She patted her huge purse in her lap. "All we have left is for him to rescue you, and for you to pretend to give him control and chase him until he catches you." She leaned around Dawn again to face Mrs. Hudson. "We might have to up our game."

"No." Dawn shook her head and stood, her knees wobbling. "No more game, no more upping. Please. I don't need rescuing, and I'm not chasing any man, even Hawk."

Mrs. Hudson nodded, approval glimmering in her faded eyes. "That's the spirit, girl. Don't let 'em know you're coming."

Dawn tried to concentrate and not scream. "Do you ladies need a ride home?"

"Of course not." Mrs. Hudson pushed to her feet. "Instead of, well *you know*, next time you and Hawk get hot and heavy, I mean if he doesn't press charges, just tease him a little. Don't give him all the goods. Just enough to make him crazy. It works with Henry every time."

Dawn backed away. "Arg."

Mrs. Poppins also stood. "Yes. Blue balls can make a man see reason and darn quick."

"I, uh, will see you later." Dawn pivoted and all but ran down the corridor, her mind filled with blue and balls. She would have to pour bleach in her ears now to get rid of what she'd just heard.

She ran into Quinn and Leila in the hallway. Leila threw both arms around her waist. "Aunt Dawn. Don't worry, Uncle Hawk is just fine, and he's not even mad at you. I made sure."

Dawn grinned and planted a kiss on the top of the girl's head. Man, she was getting so tall and so fast. "I appreciate the help."

Quinn stood apart, black eyes veiled, big and broad in jeans and a T-shirt with a badge at his belt. He reached for Leila's hand. "You and I have a lunch date tomorrow, Dawn Eleanor."

Dawn lost her smile, and her throat clogged. When her big brother used both her names, he was feeling serious. He wouldn't want to talk about her and Hawk, right? She couldn't talk about sex with Quinn. Ever. "I have work, Quinn."

He lifted one dark eyebrow, a look that had probably intimidated more than one suspect through the years. "You need to eat lunch, too."

She raised her chin and narrowed her eyes. Quinn Lodge might be the sheriff and former badass soldier, but he was also her brother and the guy who'd taught her to fight. "I'll think about it."

"Dawn." One word, said with perfect intent.

She sighed. Quinn would hunt her all over town until he found her, and then they'd have lunch. "Fine. You're buying."

He nodded. "I assumed." Then he ducked his head to look at his niece. "Leila, let's go grab something to eat. Big burgers and milkshakes."

"Awesome." Leila took his hand and led him down the hall-way. "Since it's the weekend, I don't have school tomorrow. Maybe we should go to a movie."

Dawn watched them go and then turned toward Hawk's room. Steeling her shoulders, she crossed into the room and stopped short. Her mouth went dry. "What are you doing?"

He stood, jeans on but unbuttoned, drawing a shirt over his head. The hives had already nearly disappeared. The cotton covered his delicious chest, and he smoothed back his hair, deep green eyes focused on her. "Getting out of here." He tossed the hospital gown on the bed. "I spent enough time in the hospital last year, and I ain't staying here one more second."

She wrung her hands. "I'm so sorry," she whispered.

He lifted his chin, his gaze unreadable. "Did you do it on purpose?"

"Of course not." Hurt narrowed her focus so she just saw him.

"I didn't think so. It was an accident, Dawnie. Let it go." He glanced down at his bare feet. "I don't have my boots."

No. He hadn't been wearing boots, and she'd only had the chance to grab his shirt when the ambulance had arrived. "I forgot to get the boots," she mused. Her eyes teared. "I really am sorry, Hawk."

He reached her in one long stride and rubbed a thumb across her cheekbone. "It was an accident, and I should've checked the ingredients, too. No big deal."

She shifted, heat flaring from his simple touch. "I know, but..." She felt so terrible. He could've died.

His upper lip quirked. "We both made a mistake, but if you need some punishment to feel better, I'm happy to oblige."

She stopped thinking. Her body gave a head to toe shiver that landed in a place Hawk couldn't see, but she felt. "Excuse me?" She aimed for haughty but only managed breathy.

He moved in, all heated muscle and wild scent of man, somehow even closer than before. "You torturing yourself with guilt doesn't work for me, beautiful. To feel better, you need some release. I can help you out there." One knuckle under her chin lifted her face to his. His green eyes sizzled with a predatory light, the atmosphere charging from the force of Hawk Rain. "Yes or no?"

"No," she croaked out. Who was this guy? She'd known. Deep down, she'd known Hawk owned an edge she hadn't experienced. Yet it called to her. So she exhaled, trying to appear sophisticated, "You kinky sonuvabitch."

He smiled then—a slow movement of full lips, one that turned her insides squishy and aware. "You have no clue, Dawnie. Stop feeling guilty and torturing yourself, or I'll make sure every time you try to sit down for the next week, you feel all sorts of forgiveness."

Heat slammed between her legs.

He leaned down and brushed a light kiss across her lips. "Now you're taking me home."

She turned her back to him, her heart racing. "How do you know I didn't mean to poison you?" she asked, trying for a level conversation.

His deep chuckle stirred her hair. "Because if you wanted me dead, Dawn Eleanor Freeze, I'd be dead."

She couldn't help but smile. He did know her. For the first time, she wondered how much she really knew him. Her body hummed, and her heart hammered. Yeah. She'd like to know all of him. Would he give her the chance?

CHAPTER 10

Sex should never be a weapon—always go for a cleaver. ~ The Lady Elks Secret Archives.

AN ICICLE CRASHED from the roof outside her bedroom window, and Dawn jerked awake. It was still dark outside. She lay on her stomach and stretched her hands above her head in her soft sheets, relinquishing a dream. She turned to find Hawk sleeping on his back, the covers pushed down to his waist. His features were sharper in sleep, somehow more predatory—as if he mellowed his daily look into a mask holding less danger.

Hawk Rain was all danger.

She rolled onto her side, studying the different scars across his ripped torso. They'd returned to her home the previous night, considering his boots were still tossed near her couch, and then had promptly gone to bed. To sleep.

He jerked in his dreams.

She frowned and touched his shoulder.

Hawk moved, faster than a second, pinning her to the bed, one hand banded around her neck. Her thighs widened naturally, and she clapped her hands against his ears in a resounding slap.

He jolted awake. Green eyes narrowed, and he released her neck. "Dawn. I'm so sorry. Did I hurt you?"

Her heart beat a rapid staccato against her rib cage. "No." She clutched his waist with both hands as he started to move off her. "I'm fine. I hit you hard, though."

He blinked, anger blazing red across his cheekbones. "I have bad dreams. This is why we shouldn't sleep together. I knew better."

She rolled her eyes. "Okay, Quinn Junior."

Hawk stilled, his chin lowering. "Excuse me?"

"Quinn has nightmares, too. He wouldn't let a woman sleep over for eons, until Juliet, remember?" Little tingles sparked in Dawn's abdomen and zipped lower. "He got over it. You should, too."

Hawk cocked his head to the side. "I could kill you without even waking up. How the fuck could I get over that, Dawnie?" Irritation emanated from him, heating the air around them.

She lifted a shoulder. "I woke you up with a good slap to the temple. Don't make me do it again." She held his gaze, her hands on his warm skin. "Besides, we both know that's not why you want to stay away from me." Without losing a beat, she caressed up and down his flanks, marveling at the hard-cut muscle.

"Is that so?" he asked.

The tone. Yeah. The tone held warning and just a hint of annoyance. She smiled. "You have the nightmares under control—I can tell. You're backing away from us because you're afraid we won't work out."

"I'm not backing away." He leaned up on an elbow, no longer trying to move off her. "While I'd hate to lose my best friend, you're worth the risk."

That's what she had wanted to say. "So you're all in?"

Slowly, way too slowly, he shook his head. "I'm not sure

when you started having a problem with English, but I've explained it pretty clearly."

Temper, rapid and spitting, pounded in her blood. "You don't get to kiss me, sleep with me, and threaten all sorts of kinky sexual stuff with me, and then treat me like a scared little girl." She smacked him a good one on the shoulder for emphasis.

He snatched her hand and pressed it to the bed. His gaze raked her, his eyes dark. Something, so much, lived beneath their green depths. She couldn't read his thoughts, but instinct ruled, and whatever he was thinking didn't bode well for her. Hawk's intelligence soared beyond smart to cunning and always had. He'd been gentle with her, and he'd been sweet, but at Hawk's core was neither emotion. "Do you remember when my mom died?" he asked softly.

Her head jerked, and her heart softened. Where in the world was he going with that memory? "Yes." Hawk had been in high school. "You wouldn't come live with us."

"No." He stayed on his ranch, but Loni and Tom had pretty much made him sleep over almost every night without forcing him to choose between his ranch and theirs. "Do you remember the funeral?" he asked.

Dawn used her free hand to brush hair from his face. "I do. It was a warm spring day, and the flowers were blooming every-where in yellow and purple." She'd never been so sad and had watched Hawk, flanked by her brothers and Melanie, bury his mother. Even then he'd been hard and stoic, but so much emotion had burned in his green eyes, the ones he'd gotten from a daddy he'd never met, that Dawn had barely been able to breathe. "That day changed you."

"Every day changes you," Hawk whispered. "I made everyone leave me alone by the gravesite for a little while. Remember?"

Dawn's eyes filled. "I do."

"Do you remember who didn't leave me alone?" His gaze somehow intensified.

Her throat clogged. "Me."

"Yeah. I promised everyone I'd meet them at your ranch, and they gave me space. An hour later, a pretty girl, the prettiest one I'd ever seen, walked up and slipped her hand into mine." Hawk's gaze dropped to her mouth and then back up. "We were kids. Young and hurt. I was so angry I scared everybody, even your brothers. But you walked up to me, sat down, and gave me your hand."

They hadn't talked. She'd just held his hand, staying close, offering comfort. "I know."

"That was the day, Dawnie," he said.

She wiped away a tear. "I don't understand."

"I know. But that was the day everything I had inside me, everything I'd ever be, vowed to protect you. I'd cut off the head of anybody who dared threaten you, much less harm you. Somehow, deep down, you have to get that. Yeah?" His face dipped closer to hers.

Her lungs seized. "Yeah." She was used to being protected, considering she had three older brothers who were brawlers, to say the least. "Where are you going with this?"

"I'm trying—with extreme patience, if you ask me—to explain why we're going temporarily on hold, and you're going to wait your ass for me where I want you to wait your ass for me," he said.

She frowned. "You know, I heard in high school what a bossy asshat you could be, and some girls seemed to like that. I'm not one of those girls."

"That's real unfortunate, blue eyes." He studied her, his gaze sliding from thoughtful to hungry in a span of seconds. "Let's test that theory." His lips took hers with enough force to steal the breath from her body, plundering, going deep. He took, overwhelming her, his tongue thrusting inside her mouth.

93

Her mind spun, and fire licked across her skin. She hadn't realized how gentle he'd been before. Desire scored through her, igniting every nerve as she returned his kiss. He leaned back, and she protested, her mouth seeking his, her head levering up from the pillow.

A thick band wrapped around her waist, and she found herself planted by the bed, her legs wobbling. "What?"

"Take off the shirt," Hawk said, sitting on the side, long legs extended in front of him. His large frame overtook her feminine room, his skin dark against the pale blue of her comforter. He sat, buck-assed naked with a raging erection, his gaze level on her. "Now."

She shook her head, trying to concentrate, willing her lungs to start working again. Cool air brushed across her skin, and she shivered. "Hawk—"

"I'm not asking again, Dawn. One chance here." No give showed on his rugged face, but determination glimmered in his eyes.

The look she'd seen before, every spring—one of determination and gentleness when he tamed a horse. The thought had her eyes widening and her temper flaring to compete with the desire. Oh yeah? He thought he was in control? They'd see about that. Lowering her chin, keeping his gaze, she stripped out of the T-shirt she'd donned before bed. Her breasts sprang free.

His sharp intake of breath spurred her on.

Turning her back to him, she slid both thumbs into the side of her panties and shimmied them slowly down her legs, bending over as she did so. Once she reached her ankles, she turned and glanced around her legs. "Now you can kiss my ass, Rain."

Before she got out his last name, he lunged for her, encircling her waist with one strong arm and pivoting to toss her on the bed. She landed and bounced, laughing full out. His grin flashed white and hot as he joined her, flipping her onto her stomach.

"Love to," he said, his teeth sinking into the fleshy part of her butt.

She yelped, still laughing, and tried to turn over. One large-boned hand flattened on the middle of her back kept her in place. She kicked out, only to have him settle his weight across her legs. "Hawk—" she gasped, laughing into the pillow and struggling to move.

He kissed the small bite. "You do tempt a man."

She glanced over her shoulder and blew hair from her eyes. "You deserve it."

He lifted one dark eyebrow. "So we're getting what we deserve today?"

A shiver wandered through her entire body, and his gaze darkened. "No, ah—"

With a smile, sweet and determined, Hawk Rain planted a hand across her entire ass. The slap reverberated through her skin and echoed around the room. She gasped and struggled harder against his hold, still erupting in laughter. Her breath caught as she realized she couldn't move. She *really* couldn't move.

"Where's that pretty laugh now?" Hawk asked, palming her butt and then smacking her again.

"That…wasn't…a…kiss…" she moaned.

"True." His lips caressed her warmed flesh. "Better?"

Yeah. Much, much, much better. She let out a low moan as his fingers trailed up her spine, followed by his lips. Smooth and soft, he licked a path right to the nape of her neck. "Sexiest nape I've ever seen," he murmured, pushing her hair to the side and warming her entire back. "So sweet."

She might orgasm just from his voice and the breath at her ear. "Hawk."

"Yeah." He nipped her earlobe, one hand snaking around her

rib cage and cupping a breast. Slowly, he rolled the nipple between his thumb and finger. She arched into his hand. "Hands and knees, baby."

She blinked. Apparently she didn't move fast enough, because one arm caught her rib cage and pulled up. His other hand found her, wet and wanting. Two fingers tweaked her clit, making her spasm in a series of mini-orgasms. "Hawk," she murmured, her head dropping forward.

A crinkle of foil was her only warning before he levered up behind her and grasped her hips. She took a breath, and he thrust into her. The force rocked her forward, and her fingers curled into the pillow to keep herself upright. Pleasure, so strong and powerful, filled her along with Hawk Rain.

"You okay?" His mouth wandered along her nape.

She may have whimpered.

"Good enough." Holding tight, he pushed her harder, his talented fingers continuing to torture her clit. She climbed higher and higher, her head thrown back, the orgasm rushing through her with such strength her elbows wobbled. Hawk brought her down, slowly, still fully engorged inside her.

She panted, her body shuddering.

He pulled out and turned her over, laying her on her back. Boneless, gasping for breath, she allowed him to position her. He slid both arms around her thighs, opening her, and thrust inside her again. "I want your eyes," he commanded.

She gave him her gaze, entranced by the play of muscle in his arms and chest. Sometimes she forgot. She'd known him as a kid, and she'd seen him grow, but even now, sometimes his power took her by surprise. He leaned in, holding her open, pounding hard.

Electricity zinged inside her. Her eyes widened. The feeling increased in power, flowing out, lightning fast. She grabbed his forearms. Too much. Way too much. He lifted his chin, watching her like he always had. Not missing a thing. He moved slightly to the left, barely, and pleasure rushed through her. His lids half lowered, and he did it again.

Everything inside her detonated at once, blowing her apart. She cried out, her nails digging into his arms.

He pushed harder, fucking her, finally holding tight, his body jerking with release.

"Dawn." He dropped down and kissed her, full on and hard.

She kissed him back, rubbing her palms over his damp shoulders.

Then he lifted and gave her a lazy smile.

Her heart turned over, slow and with a rumble. Hawk Rain. Inside her.

A buzz broke through her musings.

He frowned, remaining right where he was, and leaned down for the jeans discarded the night before, bringing up a phone. A quick glance at the screen had his entire body stiffening, and not in a good way. He clicked a button and held the phone to his ear. "Rain." His gaze flicked to hers, a veil drawing down.

Even with his body heating her, Dawn shivered.

"When?" Hawk asked. He waited a beat. "How close?" His eyes closed. "Keep me informed and find him. I at least need a place to start." Then he ended the call. Taking a moment, no doubt feeling her heartbeat pounding against his, he pressed one gentle kiss to her nose. "I have to get to work tracking down leads on Meyer's location as well as his storage facilities. I have guys coming to keep an eye on your place. It's overkill, since I doubt you're in danger, but we need to be safe. As of tonight, you're not staying here."

She opened her mouth to argue, to ask questions, and one hard look from him dried the spit on her tongue.

He held her gaze. "Your call, Dawn. You agree and have the day to prepare, or you go buck-assed naked over my shoulder, with no bag, right now. Decide." The sweet lover of a moment ago was gone, leaving a hardened warrior, one she didn't know, in his place.

"You said nobody knew where you lived."

"I meant that, but there's no reason to take chances. You know I transferred all of my holdings to your family before I left on the last tour, just in case, and we haven't had a chance to update the paperwork yet. Meyer knows I'm after him, so his drug buddies probably do as well, and I don't want to take chances." Hawk swept a kiss across her nose. "I'm being way overcautious, but I can't help it."

She pushed against him. "I have to go help decorate for the winter dance that's tonight. I've promised, and I also, ah, volunteered Luann and Adam. They'll kill me if I don't show."

"No," Hawk said.

She drew in air, trying so hard, unbelievably hard, to keep her temper in check. "Listen, Rain. If you can have men guarding my little cabin, you can have them guarding the Elks Building." In fact, that'd work even better, considering she needed some heavy tables moved.

"Adam's going to be there?" Hawk growled.

Dawn bit back a grin. "Yeah. We're friends. That's it."

Hawk sighed. "At least he can handle himself. Fine. I'll post the men around the Elks so you can decorate, but then you're home getting ready, under guard, and then you're with me. Afterward, you have to promise you're staying at Colton's."

"No," she said.

He grinned. "I could probably talk you into it." Slowly, he slid one finger down her cheek, over her collarbone, and across one nipple.

Electricity zapped through her. She tried to bite back a smile. "Maybe. Why don't you try harder?"

CHAPTER 11

Dress up for yourself, not for a man. He'll notice anyway. ~ The Lady Elks Secret Archives.

THEY'D WORKED for hours to transform the upstairs of the Elks Lodge into a winter fairyland that coordinated well with the existing Christmas decorations, and the room was almost finished. Sleet mixed with snow outside, slashing down, causing slush that would probably freeze before too long.

Dawn leaned back and flicked glitter onto a white tablecloth, making it shimmer blue. "Perfect."

Luann frowned and shoved her wild hair over a shoulder. Her eye shadow was a deep purple today, giving her a very cool, smoky look Dawn could never quite achieve. "Okay."

"Not everything can be pink," Dawn countered, jerking her head toward the sparkly white dust covering the bar. "I like the winter look."

"You'll like it in Paris even more," Luann countered.

Dawn grinned. "I probably would."

"You're just staying here in case Hawk wants to stay, and he's not going to," Luann countered, her eyes sizzling, her frame nearly vibrating.

Maybe. Dawn rubbed her eyes. Was she missing out on life in the hope that Hawk would come to his senses and stop courting danger? "I told you I'd think about it, and I will." She turned to where a group of Lady Elks were setting up the buffet table.

The door opened, and Adam strode in, carrying a keg. Muscles rippled in his back and arms as he marched around the bar and set it down. His dark hair was brushed back from his rugged face, and his eyes scanned the room before he visibly relaxed.

Luann hissed out air. "That man is fine with a capital F."

Dawn snorted.

Adam stood and turned, stretching his back. "Freeze? I need to talk to you." His brown eyes were veiled, and his dimples lacking.

"Ruh-roh," Luann whispered.

Dawn ignored her and crossed the room. To her surprise, Adam took her arm and led her into the back kitchen, which was empty. His hand encircled her entire bicep. She looked up. "What?" she asked.

He released her and leaned back against the door of an industrial steel refrigerator, crossing his arms. A shadow covered his jaw, and in a black T-shirt and ripped jeans, he seemed more of a rocker than a bar owner. "Explain."

She blinked. "Huh?"

His gaze narrowed, and he dug out a card from his back pocket. "Now."

Okay. Sure, Adam was a bit bossy when she was in the bar working in the band, but usually he used more than one word sentences. She took the card and opened it.

Hi Adam,

You're hot, I'm hot, and I think we should be hot together. Tonight at the dance? XOXO Dawn P.S. I love your ass.

Heat climbed into her face. She tried to speak, but nothing came out.

Adam yanked the card from her hand. "What the hell is going on?"

She looked up at him, her eyes widening. Geez. "You're mad?" Disbelief and then wounded pride slammed through her. "Seriously? If I did hit on you, you should be shockingly grateful." She had no clue what her mouth was doing, but all of a sudden, she just couldn't take any more.

He waved the card in front of her face. "You didn't send this?"

She sighed and tried to count down from five. "Of course not. I'm sure Mrs. H. did, because she wants Hawk to make a move." Jealousy, huh? Yeah. That could work.

The atmosphere changed. Adam's brown eyes warmed.

Dawn took a step back. He'd never looked at her like that. Even though her heart was elsewhere, Adam had some potency. "I didn't send that note."

He nodded. "But you did use me the other night to make Hawk jealous. Right?"

She shifted uncomfortably. "Not really. I mean, you'd already offered to take me home, and I had no clue Hawk would be at the bar." But yeah, it had worked out nicely.

Adam stepped toward her. "Listen up, Freeze. You wanna play? I'm up for playing." He ran a knuckle down the side of her face. "But I play for keeps."

She swallowed.

"If you wanna make Rain jealous, we could give it a shot, but I gotta tell you. If you're in my bed, you're not getting out." Adam released her and headed for the door. "Think about it. If that's not where you want to be, take care of this problem, and no more notes." A second later he was gone.

She shook her head. Wow. Seconds ticked by, and the door opened again. She stiffened, and then sighed as Quinn poked his head inside. "Hi," she said.

He pushed a brown Stetson back on his broad forehead. "What's wrong?"

Everything. "Nothing. Are you here to help decorate?"

"No. Let's grab lunch." He waited for her to approach and follow him, which she did with a resigned groan.

They were finished decorating, and Luann had already taken off, apparently. Adam still fiddled with the keg behind the bar, and Dawn figured they'd had enough alone time for a while. Sure, he'd just been messing with her, but even so, Adam wasn't a guy you pushed. Much.

Dawn walked outside and climbed up into the cab of Quinn's sheriff truck and waited until he'd driven out to the quiet road before speaking. Pine trees bowed under their heavy, snowy burden on either side of the road. "Did you let Hawk know the guys on duty could take off?" she asked.

"Yep." Quinn tossed his hat into the backseat.

Dawn studied her older brother. Long and lean, Quinn Lodge was all intelligence and muscle. Yeah, he was her brother, but she figured he was quite the looker. "Are you going to lecture me?"

He cut his eyes toward her before focusing back on the icy road. "Do you need a lecture?"

"Don't use that tone with me." For goodness sake. Yeah, Quinn had caught her more than once sneaking out of the house as a teen, and he'd always used that tone with her, but he'd never ratted her out. Of course, his punishment was blackmail, in that she'd always ended up mucking out stalls for him so he wouldn't tell. "I'm all grown up."

He cracked a smile. "You'll never be all grown up to me, Dawnie. But I get your point."

She shifted in her seat. If he wanted to get personal, she

could totally play. "Isn't it your turn to give mom and dad a grandkid?"

He chuckled. "According to our mother...yeah."

Dawn swiveled toward him. "Are you, ah, trying?"

Quinn shook his head. "You want to talk about sex, Dawn Eleanor?"

No, no, no. "Nope. Good point." She sat back and readjusted her seat belt. "Not at all. Never, really."

"Works for me," Quinn muttered. "I just wanted to see if you're doing all right, and make sure you're not being pushed into doing the books for the family businesses."

Dawn narrowed her gaze. "Did Luann talk to you?"

"Yes." That was Quinn. He didn't evade or even try to be smooth. "While I'd worry about you, and I'd hate to see you go, traveling Europe at your age sounds like fun."

She tried to follow his logic. "Is this about Hawk?"

"No. This is about you," Quinn said.

She reached for the button on the dash and turned up the heat on her seat. "Is there something wrong with me?" she mused.

Quinn angled her way even while taking a corner. "No. Why?"

She shrugged. "I'm not sure I want to go explore Europe right now. I've been away from home studying for so long, and now I want to be here. To play with my niece and nephews, and whatever babies Melanie has. To see mom and dad...and you guys. I want to be home." As she said the words, she settled right into them.

Quinn's dark eyes warmed. "I just wanted to make sure it wasn't because of Hawk."

"What if it was?" She knew her mind, and she knew what she wanted. "What's wrong with Hawk?"

"Nothing. I love him like a brother." Quinn drove through

the town entrance. "But he's got issues, and he's obsessed right now. Even if he comes back, he has stuff to deal with."

"Like you did?" she asked.

"Yeah," Quinn said.

Dawn bit her lip and waved out the window to some friends outside the yogurt shop. "Juliet handles your issues fine."

"Juliet is one of a kind." Quinn waved at Mr. Poppins outside the grocery store.

Dawn stiffened. "I'm not as strong as Juliet?" Sure, Juliet was all graceful and tough. But geez.

Quinn chuckled. "Baby girl, from the second you took your first step at a full run and landed on your face, only to stand right back up, I knew you were one of the strongest and most stubborn women in the entire world."

Warmth glimmered through her. "Well then."

"I'm just saying, don't plan your life around Hawk," Quinn said.

"I'm not." She leaned back, crossing her arms. "Honest, Quinn." But again, she wondered. For so long, she'd wanted Hawk, and now she'd had more than a taste of him. He was, well, Hawk. That said it all. But she didn't *know* him, not this side of him, and she wasn't even sure he'd let her love him. If not, she had to let go. Man, that was gonna hurt.

Quinn pulled into the freshly plowed parking area for the pizza shop. "I changed my mind. Lunch is on you."

She glanced around. "Oops. I left my purse at the lodge."

Quinn laughed full out. "Now that's a new one. Not."

CHAPTER 12

If a man can dance, he knows how to move in bed. ~ The Lady Elks Secret Archives.

DAWN FINISHED SWIPING on lip gloss and tugged down her short skirt. Her very short skirt. But with her cowboy boots, low-cut blouse, and sassy cowboy hat, she looked hot. Yeah, hot.

After she'd helped to decorate the Elks Lodge, she'd puttered around and worked from home, balancing ledgers for the business. Numbers made sense to her, as did music, and the correlation of those things was why she enjoyed the financial aspect of Lodge-Freeze enterprises as well as singing in the bar. But, for the first time, she began to wonder. Should she want to explore more? See the world?

She hustled into the home office to turn off the computer and glanced at the wall. Photographs she'd taken took prominence—black and whites, action shots of her family. Capturing the right moment held the symmetry of numbers for her, too. Now that she was home for good, she could take up photography again as a hobby. School had taken most of her time, and she hadn't had the chance to play behind a camera for too long.

With a sigh, she glanced out the snow-framed window to the men stationed outside. Hawk's men. He'd had them on her, watching her cabin, since he'd left earlier.

Now *there* was a man who just didn't add up neatly.

Not that she'd ever wanted him to, actually. Wildness pounded in her blood, and Hawk was her match. Most guys would've run for the hills after being poisoned. Not Hawk. He'd rocked her world and then assigned men to guard her house.

She could understand the need for men with guns, but her brow furrowed anyway. Hawk didn't see her as an equal and hadn't even asked to station guards. While she appreciated the sense of safety, he needed to work with her and not around her.

A truck rumbled down the drive, and Hawk rolled to a stop, already out of the rig before the engine died.

Wings batted through her stomach, and she took a deep breath. He rapped on the door.

"It's open," she yelled.

He stomped inside. "Why the heck is your door unlocked?"

She grinned. It had been unlocked for about five entire minutes—since she'd noticed his rig churning up snow from the road at the base of the mountain. "You have guards everywhere," she answered.

He strode into the room, arms already crossed. "You're not taking me seriously."

Holy hell. He stood in dark jeans, an even darker T-shirt, with a black Stetson perched low on his head. Broad, badass, and for the moment, all hers. His eyes glittered an untamed green, intense and knowing. Hard cut, his face angled into lines of masculine beauty only found in the wild. He lifted one black eyebrow. "Dawn?"

She smiled. "I am. Stop worrying."

His shoulders went down, and he studied his boots, obviously trying to gain some control. Finally, with an exhale, he glanced at the walls of the office, stepping closer to examine one black-and white photo from years ago. He and Colton raced horses across a spring meadow, their hair flying back, their faces intent, every muscled line of their bodies rippling with those of the animals. "I remember that day," he said.

"Me, too. It's my favorite picture, and when I get down, I look at you two. It cheers me," she admitted.

"I have one, too," he murmured.

Dawn stepped around the desk. "One what?"

He turned to her, and he paused. That gaze raked her, head to toe. Once and again.

She shivered, head to toe. Twice. Then she swallowed, her heart pounding somewhere in her abdomen. "One what?" she repeated.

Holding her focus, he reached for his wallet and pulled out a worn and dog-eared picture. "Come closer."

Her skin heated. She stepped closer, not surprised when he snaked an arm around her waist and tugged her into his side. He held a small photograph in his hand, one that had been sized down to fit in his wallet.

She had been maybe twenty, riding Titan full bore over a snowy landscape, her hat flying off, her face pink, and sheer delight across her features. Her hands were bunched in the mane, her butt off the saddle, her body free. She'd seen the bigger picture at her parent's house, knowing her mother had snapped it years ago. "Hawk," she whispered.

He glanced down at the photo. "That day, that expression, all you, Dawnie. I've wanted to ride that wildness, to hold it true, since that shot was taken."

She blinked, surprised at the tickle behind her eyes, and at the way his thoughts echoed her earlier one. "Most guys don't like that much wildness."

He tucked the picture back into his wallet. "I do. Don't want to tame it. Don't even want to mellow it. I just want to possess it and keep it close, wrap myself in it and keep it safe."

Seriously.

How was she supposed to protect herself from something like that? From a declaration like that? Possess it? Possess her? Sometimes the man spoke in a language she barely understood yet felt down deep, beyond her bones. Only Hawk. "You see the world your own way." She went to move away, and he held her tight.

He ducked his head, catching her gaze, holding it for a moment before he spoke. "Right now, you're with me, you're in my world. This means I keep you safe, and I'm hoping you trust me to do it right."

She pushed away, exasperation heating her throat. "Usually I can follow Hawk-speak, but you just lost me. Try it in English, say, from this century, Hawk."

He smiled. Slow and dangerous. Knowing. "The fact that you want modern day English tells me you read me right, blue eyes."

She couldn't quite quantify how much the statement pissed her off, or even more importantly, how to express what was wrong with it. "You're a freakin' throwback."

He chuckled. "I wish. Truth is, I'm as modern as possible. I've seen death, I've dealt death, and I've fought death. Created my own world, one I control, in order to deal. You've been on the fringe for years, as family, and I would've given my right arm for you. Now you're the center. You made it so, and you can't back out now." He turned her toward the door. "Let me at least *try* to keep you safe."

"I should've used more strawberries," she muttered, reaching for her jacket.

His laugh, full and deep, stopped her short. Masculine and beautiful…a laugh she hadn't heard nearly enough. The sound vibrated through her body in a delicious quiver.

Strong hands helped her into her coat. Her phone dinged from the pocket, and she drew it out. "Hello?"

"Dawn? It's Adam. Are you messing with me?" Adam asked.

Dawn stilled. "Um, no. What are you talking about?"

Adam sighed, the sound obviously aggravated. "Babe. Yes or no. This one looks like it's in your handwriting. Did you send me an invitation to be your date at the Elks dance tonight?"

Dawn's head jerked. "My date?"

Behind her, Hawk stiffened. "What is going on?" he muttered.

Dawn turned, sorry to see the smile that had been on his face now gone. "Um, Adam? I didn't send you an invite. Sorry."

"Didn't think so. I've given you the only warning you're going to get, Freeze. Get this under control. See you at the dance." Adam clicked off without a good-bye, in true Adam style.

Dawn chuckled and shoved her phone back into her pocket.

Hawk zipped up her jacket and drew the lapels toward him to plant a hard kiss on her mouth. "Somebody matchmaking?"

Dawn's head whirled. "Adam received an invite to be my date, which would make you jealous, theoretically, so yeah. Somebody is probably matchmaking." And she knew who. Exactly who.

Hawk rocked back on his heels. "Full truth here. Anything between you and Adam?"

"What? You didn't believe me the first million times you asked?" she asked.

He didn't respond, just waited her out.

Dawn shook her head. "Just friends. He gave me a ride home the other night because I had new snow tires being put on. Never made a move or treated me as anything other than the Lodge-Freeze boys' little sister." Like the rest of the town. Except Hawk.

"Good. I've been friends with Adam for years and would

REBECCA ZANETTI

hate to have to kill him." Hawk reached around her to open the door. "I'm leaving men on your place for the night, but I'd appreciate it if you came home with me after the dance."

She shoved into the snowy night. "See? You can take care of that attitude and ask nicely, Rain."

"I'm doing my best." He kissed the top of her head. "Though it might kill me."

* * *

THE ELKS DANCE was in full swing when they arrived. Literally. Two-stepping cowboys tossed their partners in tune with the music. Winter decorations glimmered from the ceiling, while sawdust covered the floor. A guy needed sawdust for a decent swing-dance.

Hawk didn't miss the appraising looks as he walked in with Dawn, and his gaze immediately sought out her family at the far end of the dance floor. Colton and Melanie sat at a round table decorated with glittery shit, while the rest of the gang seemed to be taking over the dance floor.

His arms itched to draw Dawn near and tuck her close.

Instead, he put a hand to the small of her back and guided her through the crowd, returning greetings on the way. Nobody seemed too surprised to see him and Dawn together.

Of course, she *had* poisoned him.

In Maverick County, that was as good as a declaration of love.

He grinned and leaned over to press a kiss to Melanie's smooth forehead. "How's the mama-to-be?"

"Huge," she said, patting her belly, a smile in her chocolate eyes. "You've obviously forgiven Dawn for trying to kill you."

He drew out a chair and waited until Dawn sat before sitting next to her. "The woman never could cook." A lie. A total lie.

Melanie snorted.

110

Colton tipped back his dark brown hat. "I have men on all three ranches, and Quinn has called in favors from other counties. We're covered."

Hawk nodded. "Good. I have a call in to Reese but haven't heard back. Hopefully he's heading this way." They were undoubtedly overreacting, but as far as he was concerned, that was just fine. Being safe rather than demolished worked for him.

For now, he was with the prettiest girl in the county, and he was going to dance. "Dawn." Standing, he grasped her arm and helped her to stand. The band was slowing down, and he wanted her against him.

She lifted an eyebrow but followed without arguing, settling into him with a soft sigh as he pulled her around. "I take it we're not hiding 'us' any longer?"

He flattened his palm over her lower back and drew her in. "You tried to kill me with strawberries, and the entire county knows about it. Hiding us is no longer an option."

She snuggled in. "What about my brothers?"

The punch to the face had already occurred, and they knew he'd keep her safe. "We're good." Hawk swung her around, drinking in the scent of woman and huckleberries. His blood hummed, and his cock hardened. "Are you good with me and now us in public?"

"Yes," she said against his neck. "So long as you realize that I'm an equal partner in everything, including dealing with psychopath killers."

The woman wouldn't know a psychopath if he showed up with flowers and spiked candy. Hawk dropped a kiss to the top of her head, enjoying her body against his. "I'm in a good mood, Dawnie. Have a soft and sweet girl against me, am surrounded by friends and family, am for once out of the crosshairs, even temporarily. Let's just pretend there aren't killers out there."

Her fingers curled into his waist, and her other hand tightened in his. "Sounds good to me. Let's enjoy the dance." She rested her face against his upper chest, her body going lax and following his.

He tightened his hold, wanting to protect her sweetness with everything he had. "I agree, but then we'll need to talk about being careful and protected for a while."

She snuggled in, again, and a sharp bite pinched into his chest. "Relax."

The minx had bitten him. The edge of pain slid through him, pulsing down to his cock. He smiled against her hair. Yeah, she was perfect. "I bite back, Dawnie. Just wait."

She shivered, her body against his, and he smiled wider. Why had he wasted so much time staying away from her? At the thought, an answer appeared, and he lost the grin. Oh yeah. Sniper, military, PTSD, and now dumb-ass drug dealers hiding from him. That's why.

But he was all in now, and they'd pretty much gone public. So all he could do was find Meyer and fulfill his promise to put the guy away. Anybody who knew Hawk, even slightly, wouldn't question his determination on that path. After he secured Meyer in prison, then he'd dismantle the entire drug operation. Hopefully he'd live through the mission, because man, he sure had something worth living for now.

His gaze caught on Quinn's. The sheriff leaned against the far bar, his arm around his redheaded wife, his eyes sober.

Hawk didn't flinch, and he didn't look away. He figured Quinn knew what he'd do, and he also figured Quinn, as the sheriff, would do his job. So be it. Hawk would deal with that if and when. For now, all that mattered was Dawn.

A tap on his shoulder caught Hawk's attention, and he turned to stare into blue eyes the exact color of Dawn's. Tom Freeze stood well over six-feet tall, still a definite badass in his sixties. "I'm cuttin' in."

Hawk handed over the man's daughter, only to be captured by a petite Loni Freeze, who stepped right into him. "You leading or am I, Hawk?" she asked, grinning up, her black eyes sparkling.

Hawk met her smile and gentled his hold. "How about I lead, and you tell me if I do anything wrong?"

"Just like old times," she said, laughing, her small-boned hand warm in his. Her light yellow dress swirled around her tall boots, giving her a feminine look that was natural to her.

"Yeah." He swung her gently, enjoying her free laugh. The woman had practically finished raising him when his mother had died, and she'd taught him to dance. "You look beautiful tonight, Loni." Not only was it the polite thing to say, it was the truth. Long black hair, sprinkled with gray, smooth skin, sharp Native American features. Loni Freeze, no matter her age, was a looker.

Just like her daughter.

She patted his shoulder. "I'm not the type to interfere, Hawk."

Somewhat true, somewhat not so much. "Yes, ma'am." He tried not to stiffen. While he loved Loni Freeze, his heart belonged to the woman's daughter, and rejection was gonna hurt. "I, ah…"

Loni smiled up at him. "All I'm going to say is that you have the right to be happy, sweetheart. I know you've had rough times, really dangerous times in the military, and I know you're torn up about that. But you're a good boy, Hawk, and always have been. If you find happiness, hold on with both hands."

His throat clogged.

The song ended, and she drew him toward Colton. "Now you mind what I said, Hawk."

"Yes, ma'am," he said, watching her turn and barrel through the crowd toward the bar, where Mrs. Hudson was laying out cookies and pretending to ignore Henry Bullton as he filched a couple. Man. The Freeze women.

They sure knew how to steal a guy's heart.

CHAPTER 13

Fight now and panic later. ~ The Lady Elks Secret Archives.

DAWN RESTED against the passenger door inside Hawk's truck, her vision hazy, her body lax. "That was a great dance." In fact, it was a freakin' dream come true. Hawk Rain, dancing freely with her, not hiding even one of his complex emotions. "Are you and my brothers okay?"

Hawk kept his gaze on the crisp snow slapping down on the truck's window. "Yes. I think. If you and I go south, there's gonna be a problem, but you already knew that. We both did."

Dawn blinked, the feeling of very nice, spiked punch warming her blood. "Why would we go south?" Besides the guy being a bossy, arrogant, overbearing hottie? She'd lived her whole life surrounded by testosterone, and she'd learned how to make her own way through that, *and* overprotective males. "No pressure here. Let's see where we go."

Hawk's phone buzzed, and he glanced down. "Mrs. Hudson needs a ride home—apparently her designated driver is drunk." He swore under his breath and turned the car around.

"I think Mrs. Poppins was her driver," Dawn said, trying not to yawn.

"That sounds about right," Hawk muttered, quickly driving back to the Elks Lodge, where both ladies stood in the outside alcove.

Hawk jumped out of the truck and opened the back door for them. "Ladies? Come get warm."

The ladies struggled through the storm, finally climbing into the backseat of the Ford with twin sighs of relief.

Hawk leaned in. "I'll go make sure nobody else needs a ride home." He shut the door and plowed through the snow to the front door.

Dawn blasted the heat. "What happened?"

"We started doing shots of tequila," Mrs. Hudson said, wiping snow off her upturned nose. "Bernie is out of practice."

For goodness sake. Dawn turned around, trying not to be impressed by Mrs. Hudson's calm voice. "How many shots?"

"Eh. Five or six," Mrs. Hudson said smoothly.

"It felt like ten." Mrs. Poppins shook out tight white curls, and then hiccupped. "I thought Henry Bullton would be headed this way because he was supposed to pick up Patty, and I just figured I'd tag along."

Mrs. Hudson nodded. "He went home with a bellyache, and I told him I'd find a ride, so not to come back."

"I didn't know that fact when I started downing shots," Mrs. Poppins slurred.

Dawn wondered if she could match Mrs. Hudson drink for drink. Probably not. "Where's Mr. Poppins tonight?"

"Hunting camp up north," Mrs. Poppins said with a grin. "Your daddy didn't go because he wanted to catch sight of you and Hawk together and figured the dance would be the place to do it."

Heat infused Dawn's cheeks. "Seriously?"

"Yep." Mrs. Poppins affirmed. "That's why Quinn got the night off, too. Didn't you feel the eyes?"

"Being watched by my brothers and dad isn't new for me," Dawn drawled.

Mrs. Hudson snorted. "Good point."

Dawn smiled. "Did you have a nice time? I saw you dancing with Henry Bullton before he went home. The man can move."

Mrs. Hudson nodded. "Yes. Henry is a very good dancer, but he's so forward, you know? We've only dated a year, and he wants to go to the next level and get all serious."

Dawn coughed. *Change the subject. Change the subject. Change* — "What level is that?" Yeah, she had to ask.

Mrs. Hudson glared through bottle-thick glasses. "You know very well what level I'm talking about, Dawn Freeze. You already reached that level with Hawk, and more than once, if I make my guess. That boy is never gonna marry you if you keep giving it away."

Dawn's mouth dropped open.

Mrs. Poppins threw an elbow into Mrs. Hudson's ribs. "Knock it off, Patty. Sex is different these days, and Hawk would be a fool not to marry Dawnie."

Marriage? Dawn swallowed. "We're dating. Just starting to date." Just because they were getting naked didn't mean they automatically would get married. Geez. Yeah, she'd always seen Hawk in her future, but she had choices.

Mrs. Hudson twisted her skinny body to face her friend. "Dawn Freeze and Hawk Rain? Are you kidding me? There's no testing the water, no *just dating*. They know that, as do their families. They're all or nothing."

Dawn slowly turned back around. The words had a ring of truth, and she shivered. Think. She needed time to think.

The driver's side door was yanked open, and Hawk jumped inside. His green gaze sought her out. "Everybody else is covered. You okay?"

"Fine," she croaked. Man. She just needed a little time to, well, mull.

"Good." Hawk glanced into the backseat. "I'll get you home safely, I promise." He slipped the gearshift into drive. "Seat belts. Everyone."

A myriad of clicks echoed through the truck, and Dawn threw a glance toward Hawk, who hadn't secured his belt. Come to think of it, he never did. Since he kept a gun at his back, maybe the seat belt put too much pressure on his torso. "Hawk? No belt?"

"Nope." He took a sharp bend and then glanced down at his phone. "Anybody you ladies need me to call?"

"Nah," came from the backseat.

A couple of minutes later, Hawk's phone buzzed. "Yeah," he answered.

His hands tightened on the steering wheel. "How bad?" Then, "Keep me in the loop." He clicked off.

Dawn's heart beat faster. "What happened?"

Hawk cut her a glance before turning back to the storm, which was rapidly gaining force. "Reese is in the hospital in Billings."

Dawn's lungs seized. "Oh no." She glanced over her shoulder to see two wide-eyed elderly women deadly silent for once. "What happened to Reese? Was it Meyer?"

"I couldn't get details, but it wasn't Meyer, because we've tracked him to the west but don't have a location. It could've been his partners, but I don't know at this point. Reese has enemies from his time with the DEA, so it could be anybody... or he could've been poisoned by a lover. That happens, you know." Despite the joke, Hawk's face lost any semblance of gentleness, and his foot pressed on the gas. "Mrs. Hudson and Mrs. Poppins? You'll be home shortly."

"Danger? Enemies of the DEA?" Mrs. Hudson struggled with

her humungous purse and drew out a well-polished Smith & Wesson. "No need to worry, Hawk."

Only in Montana. Dawn swallowed. "Um."

Hawk glanced in his rearview mirror and sighed. "Dawn? I'll take you to Colton's."

Dawn stiffened. "Where are you going?"

"Hospital. To talk to Reese," Hawk said.

Dawn nodded. "Me, too." She liked Reese, and she hated that he was hurt. "I want to see him."

Hawk didn't answer. That didn't seem good. They drove in silence through the fields and started winding up the mountain toward the more residential area. Trees lined the right side of the street, and a cliff overlooked the frozen and stunning Mineral Lake to the left.

Lights flickered around the mountain up ahead.

They reached a longer stretch of road, and Hawk leaned over to turn the heat up. Icy snow pinged against the front window.

The lights from an oncoming car cut through the haze, and Dawn held a hand before her eyes. "That moron has his brights on."

Hawk grunted in response.

"People just can't drive anymore," Mrs. Hudson grumbled from the backseat.

Dawn shielded her eyes. The oncoming car hit a series of potholes, and the glaring lights danced up and down. "Geez. Who is it?"

"Can't tell yet," Hawk said, his hands relaxed on the steering wheel. "Probably forgot about his brights."

"Flash him," Mrs. Poppins piped up.

Hawk shook his head. "No need to blind the guy."

"*I'm* going blind," Mrs. Hudson returned.

Dawn bit back a smile. "We'll pass by him soon enough." No

sooner were the words out of her mouth than the car, which looked like a newer Buick, swerved sharply across the road.

Hawk slowed.

Dawn gasped, her hand slapping against her door. "What in the world?"

The driver regained control and jerked back to his own lane.

"Just slid in the ice," Hawk returned, his gaze alert out the window. "He's back in control."

"Maybe he's drunk," Mrs. Poppins said, leaning toward the front seat.

"Maybe," Hawk said. "Or it's just icy out here, and he slid. He seems to be okay now."

Except for the bright lights, which still blared toward their truck. Annoyance buzzed through Dawn. "Those lights are dangerous."

"Humph," Hawk said.

Men. Didn't communicate worth crap. Dawn turned to glare at him.

Mrs. Hudson grabbed Dawn's headrest. "What kind of car is that?"

"Maybe a Buick?" Dawn asked, squinting to see better just as the car came closer. "I think it might be Henry Bullton."

"I told that fool to stay home," Mrs. Hudson muttered.

Suddenly, the Buick swerved again, cutting right in front of the truck.

"Hold on," Hawk muttered, yanking the wheel. The truck slid across the ice, tail swerving, as he gripped the steering wheel to regain control.

Panic flushed through Dawn, and she clutched the door handle.

Mrs. Hudson yelped and fell back into her seat.

Hawk regained control and breathed out. "We're okay—"

The Buick slammed around and nailed them in the passenger side, propelling the truck back into a wild spin.

Mrs. Poppins screamed.

Dawn jerked against her seat and flopped back, her lungs compressing. The truck spun around toward the edge.

Hawk kept in control, but the truck continued to spin, headed over the edge. "Hold on," he yelled, throwing an arm out and across Dawn's chest.

The impact threw her back and cut off her air.

Ice cracked as the truck edged over the side.

No, no, no. Dawn bit back a scream and wrapped her hand around Hawk's arm. Trees and rocks littered the way down to the lake, and there was no way they wouldn't hit one. She held her breath as they teetered over the edge and fell.

Mrs. Poppins let out a high-pitched cry.

Snow and rocks spit up, and Hawk released Dawn to grip the wheel with both hands, trying to keep them straight.

The truck fishtailed, swerved, and jumped.

Hawk jerked the wheel, turning the truck just in time for his door to impact the trunk of a smaller Ponderosa Pine. The vehicle bucked, flew, and then settled with a pop of tires.

Glass shattered.

Blood sprayed.

Mrs. Poppins screamed.

Glass smashed in from the passenger side, and the crunch of metal echoed through the night. Snow billowed down from the tree and flopped across the window. Airbags deployed with a loud hiss.

Dawn's heart beat so quickly she could barely breathe. Silence surrounded them. She fumbled for her seat belt.

"Be still," Mrs. Poppins whispered, glancing out the still intact back passenger window.

Cold and wind bustled inside the truck. Dawn slowly turned. The tree, a lone one, was the only thing keeping them from falling down the rest of the cliff. Her mouth gaped, and she turned toward Hawk.

Hawk slumped against the steering wheel and rapidly deflating airbag, not moving.

Shock stole Dawn's breath, and she tried to gasp in air, her hand on the dash. Her body launched into motion before her brain caught up, she tore free of her seat belt, and lunged for Hawk.

"Hawk, Hawk," she mumbled, his name tumbling from her lips, her hands frantically patting him. "Hawk?" Blood. Over the steering wheel and even across the front window. "Hawk?" she screamed.

He groaned.

She pulled him back, and his hat tumbled into his lap.

Silence echoed through the storm. Dawn felt for the pulse in his neck. Steady. She leaned into him, trying to see through the darkness. Blood dripped from his forehead, and his eyes remained closed. Wind and snow blew in from the broken driver's side window.

"We need to get out," Mrs. Poppins whispered. "Carefully."

She was right. Dawn took several deep breaths. Twigs and pine needles rained down, and the tree trunk cracked. "Okay. Ladies, unbuckle your belts, and slowly open Mrs. Hudson's door. You'll have to jump down." The truck lay against the tree at a slight angle.

"No problem," Mrs. Hudson said, shoving open her door with a loud grunt.

Dawn kept her hand on Hawk's pulse, which remained steady, as the elderly women scrambled from the truck. When they were safely outside, she breathed in relief. "Now just be careful climbing up the hill," she ordered.

Her door jerked open, and two pairs of faded, worried eyes gazed down. "We're not leaving you," Mrs. Poppins said.

Hawk still didn't move. Thank goodness the truck wasn't completely on its side, or she'd never get him out.

She reached up and accepted Mrs. Poppins hand. "Okay. I'll

grab him and pull." She gingerly tried to tug Hawk away from the steering wheel and to her side. The guy weighed a ton. Wrapping her hands around his arm, she pulled him across the seat, grunting with the effort. It took a three of them, using all their strength, to move his bulk.

The tree cracked loudly, and the truck pitched.

She froze. "Gently." Scooting her butt out and waiting until her feet were planted in the snow, she threw herself back, using gravity to pull Hawk the rest of the way out.

The tree splintered in two.

Dawn held tight to Hawk and fell backward, landing on her back in the snow with the cowboy sprawling on top of her.

The truck rolled over the remaining stump and plowed end over end down the hundred-yard cliff. It hit a bunch of boulders at the bottom, and the boom echoed up the mountainside.

Dawn shivered and shrugged out from under Hawk, panting in the frigid air. That was way too close.

Mrs. Poppins dragged a phone from her massive purse and started dialing. "I'll get help."

Hawk groaned.

Dawn, still sitting on the ground, pushed hair from his face. "Hawk?"

He lifted his head, and blood flowed down his temple. "Is everyone okay?"

"Why don't you wear a stupid seat belt?" she exploded.

He shoved to his hands and knees before sitting back. "So I can reach a gun if I need to jump out and fight."

"That's just stupid," Dawn muttered, standing up and swaying from the absolute relief that he was alive. "You don't need guns or fights here."

He wiped blood off his head, turning to look down the embankment. "A seat belt wouldn't have helped." Shoving to his feet, he staggered for a moment before focusing on the two elderly ladies. "Everyone okay?"

Mrs. Hudson and Mrs. Poppins huddled against a rock outcropping, snow blasting onto their white hair. They were pale but appeared unharmed. Mrs. Hudson nodded.

"I called 911," Mrs. Poppins said. "Quinn's on the way."

As if on cue, sirens trilled in the distance, and soon swirling lights came into view.

Within minutes, Quinn Lodge leaned over the road above and caused snow to cascade in a sheet down the hill. "Dawn?"

"We're fine but might need a little help climbing up," she yelled.

Silence reigned for a moment. "Okay. An ambulance is on the way, and I'll climb down in a second," Quinn said.

Hawk shook his head and winced. "I don't think we need an ambulance."

"Good. But Henry Bullton is up here in a car, and it looks like he had a heart attack," Quinn yelled back. "Phillips is performing CPR now."

Mrs. Hudson gasped and turned. "Henry!" She started to scramble up the snowy ground.

Dawn launched into motion and slid an arm around the woman. "Slow down. It'll be okay." She hoped it would be okay. The embankment was icy and rocky, but they made decent progress, with Hawk assisting Mrs. Poppins. Quinn met them halfway and made sure nobody fell.

The ambulance arrived slowly and came to a stop. The four of them reached the road just as the paramedics began to load Henry. Mrs. Hudson shuffled alongside the gurney, her little form barely visible in the strengthening storm. She clutched Henry's hand.

The elderly man was pale and unconscious but breathing on his own, thanks to the EMTs, one of whom Dawn recognized from high school. After they'd loaded Henry, Quinn picked up Mrs. Hudson and placed her inside the ambulance before turning back to them. "The EMT said that it looks like Henry had a minor heart attack and should be fine. You okay, Hawk?"

"Yes," Hawk said, wiping blood off his cheek. The red flicked down to mingle with the white snow.

"No," Dawn countered. "He was knocked out and probably has a concussion." She shivered in the cold as the adrenaline surge ebbed in her body.

Quinn glanced at all three of them. "In my truck, now. You're all going to the hospital."

Hawk shook his head. "I'm fine. Your sister saved my ass."

"Doggone it," Mrs. Poppins cursed and wiped snow off her face. "Rule number four."

Hawk turned toward her. "Huh?"

The elderly woman sighed. "No matter. Somebody take me to the hospital so I can sit with Patty."

"Of course," Dawn said, grasping Hawk's arm. "To the hospital."

"No. I'm fine," Hawk said. "We can drop off Mrs. Poppins, and then let's get out of the storm and dry off. Tomorrow morning, I need to go to the hospital to see Reese, so if my head still hurts, I'll see a doctor then."

"I'm going to the hospital to see Reese, too," Dawn muttered.

Hawk huffed just as his phone buzzed. He lifted it to his ear, listening, and didn't make a sound. "Thanks for the intel," he finally said, and hung up.

Quinn lifted an eyebrow as his deputy loaded up and jumped in the squad car. "Intel?"

Hawk smiled, the sight a little garish with the blood still dripping down his face. "A different case, Quinn. Nothing related to here."

"Right." Quinn pointed to his truck, his jaw visibly hardening. "Now. All of you."

Dawn glanced at Hawk. What had he just learned?

CHAPTER 14

Love can come at any age, and only a fool would ignore it. ~ The Lady Elks Secret Archives

THE HOSPITAL SMELLED like wet snow and disinfectant and reminded Hawk of the days he'd spent in a hospital bed for too long. Christmas decorations covered the walls, but even a jolly cutout of Santa failed to calm him. He shoved a shiver away and finished escorting Mrs. Poppins to the exit, where a deputy waited to drive her home in the darkened blizzard.

She'd sat with Mrs. Hudson for a short time, and once Henry was pronounced to be doing all right after a mild heart attack, she'd promised to return the next day. Hawk moved to the small hallway to glance inside the room where Mrs. Hudson rocked next to Henry's bed, his gnarled hand encased in both of hers.

Dawn stood outside the doorway and Hawk slipped an arm over her shoulders, his ears still ringing from the crash. "You okay?"

She nodded, her gaze on the sweet scene inside the room. "Fine. How's your face?"

It ached a little, but the bleeding had stopped. "All good." What was one more little scar in the scheme of things? He brushed damp hair away from her face and took inventory, from her wet boots to her tired eyes. "Why don't I get somebody to take you home?"

She turned. "I'd like to see Reese."

Hawk drew her away from the room and toward the quiet waiting area, not having the energy to argue. "The doctor said we can't see him for a few minutes while they do more tests, and we can't talk to the guy who was in the car with him because he's out from the morphine."

"Reese had a partner?" she asked.

"Or an employee," Hawk said.

Dawn rubbed her arms and dropped onto an orange plastic chair. "What was your phone call about earlier?"

Hawk sat next to her and took her small hand in his. "Information from Reese's crew on what they knew, which wasn't much. I hope to get more from him." None of the night was making a lot of sense, and he needed answers and now. If Meyer had found Reese outside of town, then the bastard knew where Hawk lived, which might put everyone he cared about in danger. But it was just as likely that something else had happened to Reese that had nothing to do with Meyer.

Dawn shook her head. "The doctor said that Reese and the other guy were injured in a fight outside of town. I heard them talking to one of Quinn's deputies. A fight with whom?"

"I don't know." Frustration crawled like fire ants through Hawk's gut. He couldn't relax until he discovered who'd hurt Reese.

Doc Mooncaller ambled into the waiting room, a tablet in his hands, his white coat wrinkled.

Hawk stood. "Doc? I thought your rounds here were just once a month?"

Doc glanced up from the tablet, his aged eyes focusing. With his hair braided down his back, his weathered Native American features and worn boots, he looked like he should be out riding horses and not studying charts. "We have a couple of local doctors gone at a conference, so I'm helping out."

Dawn stood and slipped her hand into Hawk's. "How are Reese and his partner?"

The simple touch somehow calmed Hawk's turmoil and let him focus. "Can I see Reese?" he asked.

Doc nodded. "They'll both be fine, although the other guy, Lenny Zonas, is out from the morphine we gave him. Broken arm, square across the left bicep. Go see Reese. Darn, but he's a cranky one. Almost as bad as you were, Hawk."

Hawk cleared his throat. "Thanks." Keeping a hold of Dawn, he maneuvered down the hallway to a room in the back. There wasn't a chance the woman would stay in the waiting room, so he didn't even ask.

They found Reese propped up in a hospital bed, bruises along the right side of his face and his right arm in a cast. Even in the bed, he looked tougher than ever. Long, lean, and muscled. His dark hair had been cut shorter than last time he'd been in town. "Is Zonas conscious yet?" Reese spat out, fury in his eyes.

Hawk shook his head and pulled Dawn into the room and away from the hall, just in case. "No. Is he in danger?" Maybe they should call the sheriff and get protection.

"Hell yes, he's in danger." Reese rubbed his bruised jaw and winced. "I'm gonna fucking kill him." He coughed. "Begging your pardon, Dawn."

Dawn hurried forward and pressed a kiss against his forehead. "What happened?"

Hawk narrowed his focus. Reese was injured on the right side, and Zonas on the left? He quickly calculated scenarios. "Are you kidding me?" he muttered. "You and Zonas fought with each other? In the car?"

"Yes." Reese leaned back against the pillows, his lips pinched in what appeared to be pain. "He's a fairly new hire, and I liked him. Turns out he's the one who has been sending information to Meyer. That's how the crew was able to break Meyer out."

Hawk lifted his head. Well, at least that was one question answered. "What else has he told Meyer?"

"I don't know." Reese scrubbed bruised knuckles down his face. "We were in the car, almost here, and something made me suspicious. The way he was asking questions. So I pulled a gun, we fought, and both ended up here."

Hawk breathed in slowly. "Does he know about me? That I live here?"

Reese focused intelligent eyes. "I don't think so. All I've told him is that I have contacts in Montana that we needed to reach, and I've never used your name."

That was good old Reese. The guy wouldn't give his own mother unnecessary information. "You sure he doesn't know?" Hawk asked.

"He shouldn't, especially since all of your land holdings are currently in the Lodge-Freeze name." Reese flexed his hand.

Hawk's shoulders relaxed. Even so, he'd have a nice chat with Zonas first thing in the morning, just to make sure.

Dawn glanced toward Hawk. "That's good, right?"

He forced a smile. "Yes. We're safe."

She smiled. "Good." Then she turned back toward Reese. "It's nice to see you here at home."

An instant smile transformed Reese from a deadly operative to a goofy guy in a hospital bed. "This isn't home. I'm just visiting."

Dawn smoothed down the bedclothes. "Right. That's what they all say. Everybody needs a home base and a place to relax, and you have that here. You feel it. Not only that, here you could have a great life, you know?"

"I like your point of view," Reese whispered, his voice begin-

REBECCA ZANETTI

ning to slur. "Sometimes you gotta take a chance at enjoying life and forget fighting death, you know?"

The words hit Hawk hard and dead center.

Reese shut his eyes. "Strong morphine."

Dawn leaned over and patted his arm. "Go to sleep. We'll be back tomorrow." She straightened and headed over to Hawk to take his hand. The movement was so natural now, he felt something in his chest ease. Finally.

Maybe it was time for him to take a chance on life. A real chance.

* * *

Dawn followed Hawk from the room, well accustomed to his way of scouting any new path before moving out of her way. He'd been a soldier, and he'd been on more than one protective detail, according to Colton. So Hawk would probably always scout the area.

Worked for her.

She also hadn't missed the expression on Hawk's face when Reese had talked about living instead of fighting death. Shock and maybe hope? Had Reese somehow, in his drug-induced chattiness, finally gotten through to Hawk Rain?

"I want to check on Mrs. Hudson," Dawn whispered.

Hawk led the way down to Henry's room, where hushed voices could be heard.

"This is it, Patty. I wanna get married before I die," Henry said, his legs moving restlessly under the blankets.

Dawn paused before entering the room. Mrs. Hudson sat facing the bed, her small form barely filling the chair but blocking Henry's face.

"You're not going to die, you old fool," she murmured, leaning forward to smooth the blankets into place.

"We're all gonna die." Henry coughed and then settled back

down. "I've loved you my entire life, Patty Hudson. In grade school, when I was away in the service, and even when you married my best friend."

Hawk pulled Dawn back against his chest, and she settled in, knowing full well they should leave the older couple alone. But something about Henry's tone and Mrs. Hudson's posture kept Dawn in place and holding her breath.

Please say yes.

Mrs. Hudson shook her head. "Love is for younger folks."

"Love is for us," Henry countered. "Please Patty. For whatever time we have left, let's share a name."

Tears pricked Dawn's eyes.

"Well." Mrs. Hudson patted his hand. "I guess I'm ready to settle down. You sure you're ready for me all the time?"

Henry chuckled. "As ready as I'll ever be."

Dawn bit back a laugh as Hawk turned her away from the door. She discreetly wiped her eyes. It looked like happily ever after had arrived for another couple in Maverick County. As she followed the stoic ex-soldier from the hospital, she had to wonder.

Would she get hers with Hawk?

CHAPTER 15

Men can get bossy, but usually we shouldn't kill them. Note: If we do decide to kill them, an alibi is a must. ~ The Lady Elks Secret Archives.

HAWK FINISHED YANKING on jeans in Dawn's bedroom, his vision clear, his head still aching. If he kept staying the night at Dawn's, he was gonna need a drawer. The sweetheart had thrown his bloody, wet, and dirty clothes in the wash the night before, after they'd left the hospital. Then they'd fallen into bed and slept like the dead.

He glanced at the unmade bed. Hmm. He'd never just slept with a woman without sex before. It had felt...right. Although sex with Dawn felt better. He grinned at the thought.

Dawn hustled in from the other room, clicking off her cell phone. "Henry Bullton is doing just fine and has announced his engagement to the entire world."

Hawk tugged on his clean shirt. "Good news. Is Mrs. Hudson still with him?"

Dawn nodded, amusement filtering across her face. "Yes. She

told the doctors they'd have to physically remove her last night, and nobody had the guts."

Well, he wouldn't try to move that woman, either. He eyed *his* woman. She'd thrown on faded jeans, a girly yellow sweater, and thick boots. Her dark hair tumbled down her shoulders, and even with minimal makeup, she was the prettiest woman he'd ever seen. Intelligence shone from her eyes, along with the spark of spirit that was all Dawn Freeze.

She blinked. "What?"

"Nothing." He brushed back his hair, wet from his quick shower. Next time, he'd carry her into the shower with him, but for now, he had work to do. "Are you ready to go to Colton's?"

She rolled her eyes. "You're being silly."

"No, I'm not. There's nothing wrong with being careful."

She put her hands on her hips. "I'm not moving until you tell me what's going on." The smell of baking muffins wafted in behind her.

He lifted his head. "Huckleberry."

"Yep, and you don't get any unless you tell me what your plan is, as if I didn't already know."

Yeah, she drove a hard bargain. He'd do almost anything for a huckleberry muffin. Thank goodness his strawberry allergy didn't extend to huckleberries. "Fine. I'm going to talk to Zonas in the hospital to just make sure he hasn't let Meyer know where I am. Now I get muffins," Hawk retorted, brushing by her and jogging into the kitchen.

Less than an hour later, they were on their way to Colton's, driving over icy roads under a blackened sky.

Hawk spent most of the journey on the phone, an irritated angel spitting at him from the passenger seat of one of his work trucks. His main truck was currently being dragged up an embankment by his ranch hands using heavy equipment and was probably totaled for good. He'd liked that truck.

Right now, he didn't care if he'd irritated Dawn. She'd be

safe, and she'd stay out of the way, just as a precaution. He hadn't been messing with her about the day at the funeral so many years ago, and now that he'd taken her, *finally*, he wasn't letting any more danger into her little world.

She was sweet, and she'd remain that way.

Hawk had to live with the fact that he may have put her in danger by coming home. Not going to happen again—and he'd do what he had to do to make sure of it. It was time to move, and now with the guy in the hospital, yeah, he'd get to the bottom of this mess. These bastards had made a *big* mistake in betraying Reese.

Hawk made the turn for Colton and Melanie's house, for once not taking the moment to appreciate the snow-covered mountains standing as sentinels around them. He drove quietly, his body settling into a stillness he recognized from battle.

Dawn crossed her arms. "I know you called the hospital this morning. How's Reese doin' in the light of day?"

Hawk slowed down to allow a gaggle of wild turkeys to cross the road. "He's pissed off and yelling at nurses, which I'm taking as a good sign." Hawk hadn't thought anybody could get to Reese.

Dawn nodded. "So he'll be out soon?"

Hawk turned to pierce her with a hard look. "He's beat up pretty bad."

Dawn's chest moved. "But he's going to be okay?"

Hawk turned back to the icy road. "Yeah." He cut his eyes to her. "Dawn, you understand that these guys are dangerous, right? I mean, I doubt they know to come here, but it pays to be cautious."

She lifted an eyebrow in true Lodge-Freeze defiance. "I know how to fight and shoot better than you think."

He knew exactly what a great shot she was because he'd practiced with her while on leave more than once. "Could you take me?" he asked quietly.

"Excuse me?"

"All bullshit aside, all ego, all feminine outrage. You against me…guns, knives, or hand-to-hand. Give me the odds." He didn't want to scare her, but Dawn had a brain made for statistics, and she'd tell the truth.

She settled back against the door. "Me and you? Hand-to-hand…with clothes on? Eighty to twenty—you."

He would've gone ninety-ten, but he had to appreciate her confidence. "Without clothes?" he asked, his lips twitching.

"Me, one hundred percent."

Yeah. He agreed with that one. "Fair enough. But here's the deal, beautiful. Your odds are based on what you think you know about me and the sides you've seen. You've never seen the side at war, and you won't. Ever." He turned into the perfectly plowed driveway. "The guys I'm after, they're not like us, and they won't fight fair. In fact, they won't fight." They'd just kill. "I know you don't get that, and I'm perfectly fine with you not getting that. But what you do need to get, and get right now, is that you're going to follow orders and stay here until I say it's safe to go home."

She rolled her eyes. "Like I said, I don't like the bossy side of you."

"Like *I* said," he said evenly, "that's unfortunate." He cut the engine, unbuckled her seat belt, and tugged her toward him to step out of the truck on his side. The hair on the back of his neck stood up, and he swept the area, finding extra ranch hands stationed at strategic points. Good. Colton had listened to him. Keeping her body between his and the ranch house, he all but carried her toward the door, which was already opening, with Colton on the other side.

It was a little over the top, but he couldn't help it. Dawn came first.

Colton drew them in and glanced around the sprawling

ranch before shutting the door. "Quinn wants you back at the station as soon as you drop off Dawn."

Hawk shook his head. "I don't need the sheriff in the way." He needed to question Reese's lying bastard of an employee, and he couldn't have anybody involved in the law there.

"How bad is Reese?" Colton took Dawn's coat.

"He'll live," Hawk said.

Colton nudged Dawn toward the kitchen, where Melanie sat sipping tea. "Go reassure Mel that you're okay," Colton said before shoving Hawk out into the cold.

Hawk braced himself for Colton's rare but formidable temper. Yeah. He'd screwed up by beginning a relationship with Dawn when things were so up in the air, and if her brother wanted to take a shot, he deserved to make it a good one.

Colton shut the door. "I have men at every station, and we're good. Quinn and Jake have to stay out of it." He turned to stride down the stairs.

Hawk paused. "What are you doing?"

Colton's shoulders went back, and on the middle step, he turned around. "I figured you'd want to talk to the guy Reese fought with, who's also in the hospital right now."

Hawk stumbled. "How did you know about Lenny Zonas?"

Colton snorted. "Like there are any secrets in Maverick County."

Hawk slid his thumbs into his jeans. "Good point."

"Then let's go. Quinn's hands are full right now, but soon he's gonna take a moment to think, and he's gonna think about you and what you're most likely doing." Colton turned and descended again, his boots throwing snow. "He's the sheriff, and he has to stop us, so we need to get a move on. Jake's a lawyer, and we're probably gonna need him, so he can't be part of it, either."

Hawk shook his head and stomped down the steps to grab Colt's shoulder. "You're not coming with me."

Colt moved then, suddenly and without warning, shoving Hawk up against the porch post. Pain ricocheted through Hawk's head, and he automatically fisted his hands in Colton's lapels.

Colt leaned in, blue eyes furious, his body strung tight. "Don't. Fuckin'. Mess. With. Me. Right. Now."

Hawk could count on one hand the times Colton had been truly mad at him during their lives, and even so, he'd never seen the dark look he was getting now. "I'm sorry everything is so screwed up. Chances are there's no danger headed this way, but I have to make sure, you know?"

Colton leaned in closer. "I know, so we're going to take care of it. This Lone Ranger bullshit you're sporting just ended."

Heat. It flared through Hawk along with panic as he glared into his best friend's face, which was way too close. "You're close enough to freak me out, Colt. If you kiss me, I'm gonna have to kill you. So how about you get off me?"

Colton shoved him away, hard. "You're such a dumb-ass right now."

Yeah, true that. Hawk was trained, and he was deadly. Sometimes he forgot Colton's training, and his time as an MMA fighter. Colt would be one excellent opponent, and Hawk didn't want to go there. Ever. "You're about to have two babies," he said slowly.

Colton slid his hat further up his head. "I was there for the last doctor's appointment, Hawk. You're not tellin' me anything I don't know."

"So stay here and keep your woman safe." *And mine, too.* He didn't say the words, but they certainly filled the air around them.

"I've got good men on them, and Jake's on his way here. So you and I are doing this. No more *alone* crap, and no more chances." Colton pivoted and strode toward Hawk's truck. "If you're not at the truck when I am, I'm taking it."

Hawk shook his head, caught between being pissed and grateful. "Colt—"

"You're another brother to me, Hawk. You know it, I know it, and Quinn will know it. So let's go do what we gotta do and keep him out of it. It's the least we can do." Colton hitched into the truck.

Hawk gave up. When Colton Freeze set his mind to something, nobody, and that meant absolutely nobody, would stop him. "Fine. But if it gets illegal, and it's gonna get illegal, you let me break the law."

Colton rolled his eyes. "Shut up, and think about one thing for a moment—it wasn't your fault Meyer stabbed your buddy. Stop feeling guilty and just live your life."

Hawk recoiled like he'd been punched. Was that his mindset?

They didn't talk on the way in, both lost in thoughts, both pissed off. Anger swelled in the truck, cascading around, at home and not going anywhere. Hawk figured they should probably talk about Dawn, but now wasn't the time.

They reached the hospital and slipped in the back door behind an orderly returning from a smoke break. "I called Junnie Allice earlier to get the guy's room number." Junnie Allice ran the florist shop in town and knew everyone at the hospital. Hawk didn't know who she'd called to get the room number, and he didn't care. "Room two eleven."

Colton nodded.

It occurred to Hawk that he'd seen some shit, Colton had seen some shit, but they'd never actually seen shit together. They'd always had each other's backs, though. On the football field, the baseball diamond, even back alleys after bar fights.

They found the room and then quickly backed around a corner. A Maverick County deputy stood outside the room, holding up the wall.

Colt rubbed his whiskered chin. "Quinn isn't stupid."

No. The sheriff was nowhere near stupid. Hawk scrubbed both hands down his face. "That guy new?"

"Yeah. I think his name is Chuck. Or George." Colton shrugged. "He doesn't know us, and he'll have orders from Quinn, who he does know. We're screwed. Any ideas?"

"Besides blowing up my truck in the lot as a diversion?" Hawk whispered. "No. Besides, if Quinn is onto us, then he's told the deputy not to move...no matter what." He eyed the far door. "Remember last year?"

Colt tipped up his head. "Yeah. When we jumped out the window." It could work. "Chances are the window isn't unlocked though."

Hawk's spine straightened, and he nudged Colton aside. "There's only one option, and you can't be a part of it."

Colton shook his head. "There's no choice."

Hawk eyed the distance between the deputy and him. Running would draw attention, and stealth would take ten long strides. "There are no cameras in the halls, although there was one in the entryway. We could say we were visiting Reese. We need a way to knock the deputy out without him seeing us. One of us could distract him, but Quinn will know it's us."

Colton shrugged. "Quinn's going to know it was us no matter what. The issue is *proving* it, and we have to make sure he can't. If for nothing else, then to protect him."

Hawk nodded. "Good point."

Colt cut him a look. "You distract the cop, and I'll have a talk with the patient."

Hawk shook his head. "No. This guy's mine."

"Fine. Give me a few." Turning, Colt jogged out the back door.

Hawk took several deep breaths—his hands steady, his head wound still pounding. What he wouldn't give for a week on a beach with Dawn just to play and explore whatever they had going on. But right now, he had to break the law and scare a guy in order to keep everyone he cared about safe.

So much for leaving violence behind.

He'd only been seeing Dawn a few days, and she'd already been in a car wreck—and had actually saved his butt the previous night. Pride, unwelcome and irritating, slid through him. His girl had stepped up, now hadn't she?

Colton's voice came from down the corridor. "Dude, I'm the sheriff's brother, and he sent me to talk to the guy in this room. You need to get out of my way."

Hawk peered around the corner to see the deputy facing Colton, hands at his hips, shaking his head. The hallway was quiet with no witnesses. The cop reached for his phone, and Colton grabbed for it. "Mr. Freeze, I have to ask you to stand down."

Hawk moved silently and grasped the guy in a headlock.

Colton feigned a gasp, his eyes widening on Hawk, his hands going up in fake shock. "Who are you?"

The deputy scuffled, and the guy had bulk. Hawk held on tight, grimacing, finally relaxing when the deputy lost consciousness. "Quinn's going to kill us," he muttered, settling the deputy in a fluorescent orange chair and adjusting his cowboy hat over his head.

"Yeah." Colton sat next to the guy. "Hurry up, so I can call this in like I actually witnessed something."

Hawk dodged inside the room and stalked patiently toward the bed. The guy was in his early thirties, long brown hair, scruff across his chin, body gone partially to fat. His eyes were open, and alarm filled them. He reached for the call button, and Hawk knocked it out of his hand.

Leaning in, Hawk placed a hand over the man's neck. "You have a millisecond, so listen up. You put a friend of mine in the hospital, and you put in jeopardy everything I care about, which means you should die. Killing you wouldn't bother me much, but it'd put my friend, the sheriff, in a spot, so if you work with me, I'm gonna let you live." To emphasize his point, Hawk slid his hand up to cover the man's mouth and nose just long enough to cut off all oxygen.

The guy went still.

"Do you get me?" Hawk asked.

The man nodded, and machines around them beeped rapidly.

"Where's Meyer and what does he know?" Hawk asked.

CHAPTER 16

Men want an angel in public, a mom in the kitchen, and a wildcat in bed. Do NOT *get those mixed up.* ~ The Lady Elks Secret Archives.

DAWN MOVED from Melanie's bright kitchen into the large gathering room, where a fire crackled in a massive stone fireplace near a seven-foot Christmas tree decorated in bright colors. The teapot she carried was vintage, as were most of the furnishings and even the drapes across the wide windows. The entire effect was country, homey, and comfortable.

The snowstorm had finally stopped, and the sun shone down to reflect off snowy fields.

Dawn refilled Melanie's teacup and tried to smile. "Why are men such dumb-asses?"

Melanie shrugged and sipped her tea, sitting back on a muted suede sofa that added a calmness to the woodsy living room. "I think it's something in the excess testosterone." She stretched her feet out on a matching ottoman. "I could be wrong."

Dawn snorted and placed the pot on a wide serving tray her mom had given Melanie for a wedding present. "I think you're right. How are you feeling, anyway?"

Mel rubbed her huge belly. "Fantastic, in an *I swallowed volleyballs* kind of way. Excited for the babies to get here."

Dawn sat. "Why haven't you had the ultrasound to find out the sexes? I want to go shopping."

"I like surprises." Mel chuckled, her brown eyes laughing. "Colton does not. Therefore I won." She set down her cup and shoved curls off her forehead. "So. I guess it's time we talked about Hawk, right? How are things?"

"Crazy. He's pissed that Reese was hurt, and I'm not liking the pressure from all around. That just because we started dating, it means forever." Dawn took a sip and scalded her tongue.

Mel nodded. "Yeah, but with you and Hawk, didn't you figure on forever?"

"Yes." Dawn lifted a shoulder and set down the offending mug. "I've known Hawk my whole life, but I didn't really *know* him, know him. You know?"

Melanie lifted an eyebrow. "Sister, I'm one of the few people alive who actually would understand and agree with that statement. Colt and I were friends forever, but when we, ah, you know, things totally changed. *He* totally changed."

"Exactly." Dawn leaned forward, her breath rushing out. "Hawk's always been a sweetie, not a chauvinistic dick who ordered everyone around. Sure, some of that's from the military, but the other part? That's just because we bumped uglies and now his main goal in life is to keep me from getting shot."

"I have to be honest in that I think that's a good goal." Melanie blew on her tea. "However, I agree about the bossiness. That can't be allowed to continue. Getting your brother to back off was tough."

Dawn swallowed a grin. Colton hadn't backed off. Not a bit.

In fact, he was even more protective since Melanie had gotten pregnant.

"Shut up," Mel said without much heat.

"Didn't say a word." Dawn reached for her cup again.

The front door burst open, and she jumped. Colton stomped inside with Hawk on his heels. She half rose.

Colton reached his wife and planted a hard kiss on her lips.

Dawn faltered and then sat down. "Um—"

The trill of sirens, somehow angry, violated the quiet winter morning. Oh no. Dawn stilled, and her stomach dropped.

A truck roared to a stop, heavy boot steps clanged on the stairs, and then Quinn Lodge stood inside the room, a swell of anger cascading from him and heating Dawn's lungs.

His hard gaze took in both Hawk and Colton. "Out. Side."

Another truck came to a stop in the driveway, and everyone paused. Seconds later, Jake Lodge strode through the doorway. "What the holy fuck of a holy fuckup of a fuck were you two fucking fuck-ups fucking doing?" he yelled.

Melanie snorted and dropped her face to her cup, her shoulders shaking with laughter.

Dawn's mouth opened and shut, but she couldn't find words.

Colton turned toward his oldest brother and instantly took a square-on punch to the jaw from Jake. He fell into Hawk, who righted him. Then Colt lunged for Jake.

Hawk slipped in front of Colton, and Quinn punched hard and fast. Hawk flew back into Colton and then sprang forward and into the sheriff.

Melanie stood, holding her stomach. "Knock it off. Now."

All four men froze.

Hysteria bubbled through Dawn, and she gulped it down.

Quinn recovered first. "Hawk Rain and Colton Freeze. You have the right to remain silent—"

Jake faced off with the sheriff. "Probable cause?" he barked.

Quinn turned toward Jake, fury darkening his rugged cheek-bones. "Seriously?"

"Wait a minute." Hawk tried to step between them. "You two don't fight."

"Shut up," they said in unison.

Jake stepped into Quinn's face, both of them tall, broad, dark, and furious. "Listen, sheriff. I want nothing better than to beat the crap out of these two, and don't think I won't, but you don't have probable cause for an arrest."

Quinn shifted until they were nose to nose. "I do. I have these two morons on camera entering the hospital, and Colton witnessing whoever knocked out my deputy. So feel free to follow me to the station, counselor."

"They could've been visiting anybody, and that's not probable cause," Jake shot back.

Dawn swallowed, and her arms trembled. Anger. Way too much of it surrounded them. She shuffled to her feet. "Can we just talk about this?"

Colton reached for his wife to settle her back in the chair. "Listen. This is what happened—"

Jake whirled on him in unison with Quinn. "Shut up," they both growled.

Dawn would've laughed had it not been so scary. "I, ah…"

Hawk's head pivoted, and he silenced her with one hard look. "You know absolutely nothing and have nothing to add."

Quinn sighed. "I agree. Now you two dipshits get your butts in the back of my rig. We have to sort this out at the station, away from Dawn and Melanie, because none of this touches them."

The door pushed open, and Reese Johnson leaned against the doorframe, a hospital gown barely covering him, big fur-lined black boots up to his knees.

"Reese?" Quinn breathed, catching his tall friend before he hit the floor. "How?"

Reese smiled wanly and allowed Quinn to help him inside the room. "I, ah, may have borrowed a car from the hospital." He shook snow out of his dark hair. Bruises covered his face, and bandages blanketed his muscled arms. "I thought I should let you know that Colton and Hawk visited me at the hospital. Hawk stayed with me the entire time. All morning. Just in case a camera caught them coming into and then leaving the hospital."

"You've lost your mind." Quinn grabbed a blanket to toss on his friend. "You're providing an alibi for these two morons?"

"Yes." Reese leaned back with a tired groan. "I heard a deputy was choked unconscious, and I also heard he didn't see who did it. But my former employee, the one being guarded, hasn't had anything to say, so we just don't know who went inside to chat with him."

Quinn growled. "I know he hasn't talked, because I tried to *get* him to talk. Seemed a bit scared."

Reese shrugged and then winced. "Yes."

"The deputy was talking to Colton when he was choked out," Quinn hissed.

Jake shook his head at his youngest brother. "My client didn't recognize the guy who choked out your deputy, and he has nothing to say to you. The fifth and all that."

Somehow, although it seemed impossible, Quinn's anger swelled hotter and higher. "This is not okay," he snapped through gritted teeth.

"Totally agree," Jake said, cutting a hard look at Colton and Hawk. "The law isn't going to deal with these two."

Quinn smiled then, and it wasn't pretty. Not by a long shot. "That would leave us, then."

"Yes." Jake nodded. "Now, Sheriff Lodge, since you lack probable cause to arrest my bonehead clients, I ask that you leave us alone to talk."

Quinn's chin lowered.

Jake's lifted. "You're the sheriff, Quinn. You have to go."

"You can't be here, either," Colton said quietly.

Jake leveled him with a look. "I'm under an obligation, as an officer of the court, to report any bodily harm crime one of my clients is planning to undertake. Since I don't have a client about to break any law, I can be here. Got it?"

Both Colton and Hawk held firm, their expressions not giving an inch.

Reese cleared his throat, his gaze on Hawk. "My men have intel, or they will soon, about a drug storage facility outside of Wyoming. When they get the info, I need to go in and finish the organization. Even if Meyer is long gone, we can hurt him by dismantling everything he has built. You in?"

Hawk stilled. "Yes."

A muscle pounded in Quinn's jaw. "Reese? I have no doubt you haven't been released from the hospital. Get up, and I'll take you back." Quinn eyed Jake. "If you get any news, if anybody goes anywhere, I expect a phone call." He turned to Hawk. "Let Reese's men handle Meyer. He's probably out of the country, and you can just stay here."

"Yes, sheriff," Hawk drawled.

Melanie cleared her throat. "Ah, Reese? It's nice to see you here in Maverick County."

Reese grinned. "Thank you."

She rubbed her belly, her gaze going from the serious brothers to Reese. "Doesn't he fit right in?"

Reese chuckled. "I am *not* moving to Maverick County."

"Famous last words," Melanie said with a smile.

Jake clapped Quinn on the shoulder. "Give Dad a call, Quinn. He's probably heard about everything and will be heading this way if we don't reassure him."

"Fine." Quinn glanced at Dawn. "She stays out of it. Any of it."

"My word." Hawk's posture straightened. He and Quinn

shared some man-look that did nothing but irritate Dawn, but enough was enough, and she kept quiet for the moment.

Reese met Quinn at the door, and Quinn swung under his friend's arm to help him to the car. "You're as dumb as the rest of them," Quinn could be heard grumbling before the front door closed.

Jake turned to eye Colton and Hawk. "Well? Where's Meyer and does he know Hawk lives here?"

* * *

DAWN PACED BY THE FIREPLACE, her mind spinning, her stomach lurching. The guys had left shortly after noon, and they hadn't called through dinner or even after. It was almost ten at night, and having no word from them was about to kill her.

Melanie sat behind her, quietly contemplating the crackling fire.

"How can they still be at the sheriff's station running down leads?" Dawn muttered for at least the tenth time.

Melanie shrugged, appearing calm, but lines cut into the sides of her mouth.

A knock sounded on the door, and Dawn hustled to open it. She stood to the side—okay, so maybe some of Hawk's wariness was rubbing off on her—and checked the peephole. On the porch stood one of Hawk's ranch hands, loaded for bear, along with Mrs. Hudson and Mrs. Poppins. She undid the locks and dragged open the storm door.

"Oh my. Men with guns," Mrs. Poppins twittered, pushing inside, a crinkling brown bag in her hands. Her track outfit was lime green with orange sparkles, and even her puffy white coat had been bedazzled down one arm. "We had Kurt drop us off on his way home from making coffee."

Dawn helped Mrs. Hudson, who glittered even more than

Mrs. Poppins, inside before nodding to the ranch hand. His lips twitched, but he closed the door.

"Let me take your coats," Dawn said, manners drummed into her from day one. She took both jackets and hung them on hooks by the door. Mrs. Hudson set down a big bag in order to hand over the coat, and then picked it back up. "How is Mr. Bullton?"

"Stubborn as a bull." Mrs. Hudson smiled widely. "But he gets to come home tomorrow. I may, ah, stay over and help him to recuperate."

Dawn hid a smile. "That would be mighty nice of you."

Melanie struggled to reach her feet. "May I offer you ladies some tea or cookies?"

"No." Mrs. Hudson waved Melanie back down. "You sit, dear. The babies will be here soon, and you'll forget how nice it is to sit." She turned, a glimmering vision of vibrant purple. "We brought some gifts for Dawn."

Dawn swallowed and waited until the ladies had taken seats before sitting. They'd probably brought more food. "I can't give Hawk food and pretend I made it." If nothing else, the guy knew her cooking.

Mrs. Poppins sadly shook her head. "Oh, honey. We're past the rule about trying to get to his heart through his stomach."

Mrs. Hudson set down her bag and cleared her throat. "Nearly killing him took the bloom off that rose."

Melanie coughed. "Um, what's going on?"

Mrs. Poppins swung toward her. "Dawn hasn't told you about our plan?"

Mel cut her a look and then shook her head. "Ah, no."

Mrs. Poppins twittered and dug in her shiny jean purse to draw out a photograph. "We stitched this pillow for Dawnie so she'd know how to get a man. More specifically, Hawk. It's time that boy settled down."

Melanie took the picture and read. She pressed her lips together. Tight.

Dawn breathed in evenly through her nose, trying to avoid panicking. If Melanie laughed, Dawn would join in, and she wouldn't be able to stop. "I've broken almost all the rules," Dawn said, trying to keep the laughter at bay.

Melanie smiled, her body shaking just enough. "You've broken them all."

"Not the last one," Mrs. Hudson countered. "You can still give him control and then chase him 'til he catches you. Trust us." Her bony fingers wrapped around the brown bag.

Dawn stilled. "Um."

Mrs. Poppins stared out from coke-bottle glasses. "Now, a good sex life is nothing to be ashamed of, Dawn Freeze. Even if you did start too early with Hawk and not wait for the ring. We can fix this."

"We surely can." Mrs. Hudson reached into her bag and drew out some bright red straps with a harrumphing flourish. "These are, um, restraints." She peered closer to read a tag on one end. "I think they go under the bed and have cuffs."

Melanie lost it. Holding her belly, she threw back her head, and her entire body gyrated with laughter.

Dawn's mouth dropped open, and she started to pant. This wasn't happening.

Mrs. Poppins frowned and squinted. "Surely you've read current romance novels, dear."

Dawn slowly shook her head. "No, ma'am. Not lately." The straps were red and looked strong.

Mrs. Hudson placed them on the couch and reached into the bag again.

Dawn couldn't help it. She leaned forward, morbid curiosity propelling her. "Where did you ladies get this stuff?"

"Sex shop north of Billings," Mrs. Poppins said, smiling

when Mrs. Hudson brought out a large, black, bulbous looking thing. "Now that's kinky."

Dawn frowned. "What is that?"

"Butt plug," Mrs. Hudson said.

Melanie's laughter increased so hard she shook the entire couch. Pillows fell to the floor.

Dawn's ass clenched. "Oh, not a chance." No way would that fit in somebody's butt. "That's crazy."

Mrs. Hudson held the bulb up and frowned. "Maybe you're supposed to start with a smaller size."

"Oh God, oh God, oh God." Tears actually coursed down Melanie's face.

Dawn cut her a hard look. "I can't, I mean, this is, I, ah—"

Mrs. Poppins pulled out a paddle. Bright green with hearts cut into it, the word SPANK ran down one side. "This looked kinda pretty."

Dawn sat back, her mind spinning. Melanie slapped a hand over her mouth but continued to snortle over it.

Mrs. Poppins whacked the paddle against her brown-spotted hand, and Dawn jumped. "This could do some damage." The elderly lady squinted toward Dawn. "Do you think Hawk knows how to spank a girl? We wouldn't want him to hurt you."

This wasn't happening. It really wasn't.

Mrs. Hudson smacked Mrs. Poppins on the arm. "Of course Hawk knows how to spank a girl. I mean, it's *Hawk*." She arched white eyebrows. "Right, Dawn?"

Dawn made a strangled sound. Heat flared into her cheeks, and her eyes actually stung. "I can't believe this."

Mrs. Hudson pulled out a plastic covered package. "This is a pocket rocket. Now, it's for clitoral stimulation." She nodded solemnly. "That's important, you know."

Dawn dropped her head to her hands. "Kill me. Just kill me."

A knock sounded on the door. "Melanie, it's Quinn." His deep baritone wound through the night.

Panic ripped through Dawn, and she lunged for the bags, shoving everything inside them. No way could Quinn, her older brother, see this stuff.

The elderly ladies helped her pack up, twittering anxiously.

Melanie snorted. "Throw the bags in the guest room. Hurry."

Dawn ran into the room to toss the bags on the other side of the bed. She returned just in time to see Quinn stomp inside. "Hi," she said.

"I got notice from one of Hawk's men that Mrs. Hudson and Mrs. Poppins were visiting. I'm here to take them home." He frowned, studying his sister. "You okay? You're flushed."

Yep. She could die just right there.

CHAPTER 17

Love can't work without trust—make sure you give and get that. ~ The Lady Elks Secret Archives.

AN HOUR after Quinn had taken the crazy elderly women home, Dawn curled up on the couch, her gaze on the fire. Her fingers played with the soft silk scarf around her neck. It matched her sweater and made her feel more put together. "Have you ever seen a butt plug like that?"

Melanie chuckled. "No. I just wish I could've been in the store when they'd gone shopping. Can you imagine?"

"No." Dawn didn't want to imagine. Ever. Quinn had taken the ladies home, and Dawn had made a quiet dessert for Melanie, who was having all sorts of aches and pains, probably from laughing so hard earlier. "I wish the guys would get home."

The sound of a truck finally echoed up the drive.

Minutes later, the door opened, and Colton tromped inside, followed by Hawk.

"We think we traced a private plane to Canada, of all places,"

Colton said without preamble. "Meyer headed north instead of south. We lost him there, although I'm thinking he moved on."

"I guess Zonas was telling the truth," Hawk said, nudging the door closed. "Meyer is long gone."

"It makes sense." Colton shook snow from his hair. "You guys won't stop hunting him, so why not get a good head start?"

Dawn shivered.

Melanie tugged Colton down to sit on the couch. "Enough of this, guys. We have a right to know what's going on."

Dawn lifted her chin and crossed her arms. "Fill in all the blanks and tell us the entire story. Now."

Hawk eyed Colton and then grimaced. "Meyer was an explosives expert on my first tour. He was a great soldier who discovered a fast way to make money by funneling drugs. I caught him and turned him in. Unfortunately, he was brought home to be tried, and he escaped." Hawk tugged out a worn picture of three soldiers with whom he'd served. "Meyer is in the middle." About six feet tall, brown hair, dark brown eyes. "He could've done anything and instead chose to run drugs. The guy next to him was a friend of mine who Meyer stabbed. I promised I'd make things right."

"Meyer put you in the hospital last year?" Melanie asked.

Colton rubbed her belly and shook his head. "No. Apparently that was Meyer's guys, but not him. He was elsewhere, and we're not sure where yet."

Hawk shook snow off his jacket and unzipped it to hang by the door. "Reese hired me eight months ago to find Meyer."

Dawn frowned. "Wasn't the government looking for him?"

"Yes, but certain contacts in the government were all right with hiring outside contractors who weren't, ah, restricted by the constitution. Or laws." Hawk pushed up the sleeves of his green shirt. "I found him and brought him in, thinking that would be it. But he always was a talented sociopath. He escaped custody and now is on the run."

Dawn shook her head. "So the guy in the hospital gave you his current location, which led you to Canada, and now he's gone."

"Long gone," Colt said.

"So we're in the clear?" She focused completely on Hawk.

"I hope so. When I took him in, it wasn't pretty." Hawk reached to the side and locked the door. "I'd feel better if we stayed vigilant until we catch him, just in case. I've sent a rotation of ten men to watch your folks, five to Jakes, and they'll rotate tomorrow to watch this place. We have two men scouting outside here tonight. Quinn is working, so Juliet is at Jake's. We're covered for now."

Melanie struggled to her feet, frowning when Colton had to give her a gentle push. "You guys hungry?"

"No. We caught something on the way home." Colton stood and took her hand. "Let's get some sleep."

Melanie turned to Dawn. "Guest room is off the kitchen."

Dawn knew that, considering she'd stashed the sex toys there earlier. Geez. Her face heated until her cheeks hurt. Besides, her older brother was in the room, and he knew she was going to share a bed with Hawk.

Melanie bit her lip and obviously avoided looking at her husband. "Awkward," she mumbled.

Colton turned toward the stairs, definitely not meeting anybody's eyes. "Woman, you're a pain in my ass," he muttered, a smile in his voice. "Let's get some sleep while we can."

They disappeared upstairs, and Dawn hugged her arms around herself. "Well."

Hawk didn't move her way. "Well."

She swallowed as tension, all Hawk-like and masculine, wandered over and licked her skin. "It's weird, right? You and me, here at Colton's." She started babbling and couldn't stop. "I mean, we've stayed together, all of us, before, but—"

"Dawn." The green of his eyes darkened to a hue holding danger. "Come here."

She didn't take orders well, if at all, and so when her body kicked into gear, her mind barely had time to catch up before she reached him. She faltered, and he snaked out a quick arm to tuck her into his side. Dawn drew in his scent. Yummy, masculine, and free. She smiled against his shirt. "So. What now?"

* * *

HAWK SWUNG HER UP, smiling at her surprised *eek*. Dawn filled out his arms nicely, all womanly curves and warmth. The idea, the very idea, that she had to hide out from a drug dealer in order to protect him pissed him off until he couldn't see straight. So he set it aside, holding onto what mattered.

Dawn Eleanor Freeze.

All woman, all brain, all sass. She was the entire package, and she was smart enough to know it.

But she didn't know him. Not all of him.

He carried her through the living room and into the guest room, one he'd stayed in more than once. A hand-stitched coverlet, older than them both, covered a sprawling bed that was piled high with pillows. Melanie loved pillows and always had.

Holding Dawn with one arm, Hawk swept the majority of the pillows to the floor. "Now we have a minor discussion, a little argument, and then I'll make you come hard enough you forget you're pissed at me." In a move that made her gasp, he flipped her around and took her shirt and pretty scarf with him.

She landed on her back, eyes wide.

Yeah. He could be smooth. His chuckle matched hers, even as his body began to tighten. Dawn Freeze, in a pretty bra and jeans, spread out on a bed. Two strides took him to the door so he could engage the lock.

Even not touching her, he could see the shiver wind through her sweet body.

"Why are we going to fight?" she asked.

He liked that she made no effort to cover the lacy white bra or her bare midriff. He liked it a lot. "All of the Lodge-Freeze women are taking a nice spa vacation starting tomorrow."

She blinked.

He slowly began unbuttoning his shirt, waiting for the explosion.

"Who's payin'?" she asked.

He lifted an eyebrow. "I'm fine footing the bill." Although Reese had offered to cover the expenses from his company. "So you're going?"

She rolled to the other side of the bed to stand. Something crinkled, and she shifted to her feet. "No."

He dropped his shirt to the ground. "Wrong answer."

She lifted a smooth, very creamy, and delicious looking shoulder. "I'm not going anywhere, and I doubt my sisters-in-law are, either. We're not the type to run and hide from a fight, Hawk, and you know it."

His body clenched. "The fact that the fight might come to Mineral Lake is my fault, and I'll take care of it."

Color bloomed beneath her fine cheekbones, hot enough to burn, if he had to guess. "You're stunning when you're angry," he whispered.

"Then I'm about to be fucking gorgeous." She pressed both hands on her hips.

He shook his head. "There you go with that mouth again." She was amazing, and he really wanted to— His pocket buzzed, and his shoulders stiffened. Keeping her gaze, he drew out his phone and read the text. Then he read it again. "Dawnie?"

"Yeah?" Attitude echoed in her tone.

"Do you have a bag of goodies for me?" He lifted his head, fascinated when red burst across her sassy face. "Dawn?"

She coughed. "Um. No."

He glanced back down at the phone. "Mrs. Hudson just texted me, emoticons and all, saying to make sure you give me my bag of goodies." He was hungry, but not for cookies. "Did she bake?"

Dawn's head lifted. "Yep. She baked. Definitely baked. But Melanie's knocked up, and we, ah, ate all the brownies. I'm sorry."

His phone buzzed again, and he read the text out loud. "She said there's a brown bag on the other side of the bed."

Dawn backed away until her butt hit the windowsill, pure panic trembling her lips. "Nope. No bag. Sorry." Her eyebrows lifted and she jumped for the bed, landing on her knees. "Why don't we continue the fight naked?"

His interest was piqued right along with his cock. "You first," he murmured. What was in the bag?

Dawn patted the bed, apparently having forgotten about their fight, although she *was* fucking gorgeous. "Why don't you come help me?"

He crossed the room and put a knee to the bed, reaching out and flicking her bra open. Front-clasp bras were the best invention in the last century. She gasped and glanced down. "Not your first rodeo."

Amusement and desire warmed him throughout. "No." Grasping her waist, he lifted her until she stood and quickly tore down her pants before settling her on her back.

She chuckled. "Man, you can move."

"Just wait." He straddled her, the need to possess trying to silence him. "What's in the bag, Dawnie?" he whispered.

"Nothing." Her face flamed again.

Interesting. He leaned to the side, and bright red straps spilling out of a grocery bag caught his eye. "Are those…"

She gasped and covered her face with her hands. "Restraints.

Yes. Mrs. Hudson and Mrs. Poppins thought I could catch you if I got kinky."

He stilled, his mind spinning and then discarding all thoughts of the elderly women and sex toys. "I kinda wish I didn't know that."

Dawn lowered her hands. "Me, too."

Her breasts were high and full, her nipples already hard. The back of his hand swept across them, and fire licked down his spine to his balls. "I wouldn't use ties like that."

She smiled, confidence beginning to shine in her eyes. "I figured."

He reached for her discarded scarf, enjoying the feel of silk across his hand. "I'd use something much softer for your sweet skin."

* * *

DAWN STOPPED BREATHING. His hands, large and formidable, caressed the flowered scarf. Dark eyes, green and fathomless, studied her. His jean-clad thighs trapped her hips on either side, and warmth from his body swelled toward her. "You're joking," she managed to croak.

He smiled then.

It was not a sweet smile. Nor an amused one. The curve of his lips promised something...new. "Joking? I am." He reached for her wrists. "Not."

Hunger snaked through her with a sharpness that stopped her breath. She struggled, and he easily wrapped the silk around her wrists, drawing up. He had to lean over, his chest brushing hers, in order to tie the material to the iron headboard.

He levered back. "Interesting. I've stayed in here a million times, and I never really studied that headboard."

Dawn tugged and her hands remained in place, her arms over her head, her back arched. Warmth heated between her legs. She couldn't move. Captured. The red restraints on the floor seemed silly, harmless compared to unrelenting band of silk constraining her.

He ran his hands over her chest, rolling both nipples.

Electricity jarred her, and she moaned.

"What else is in the bag?" he asked.

She tried not to blush. "You don't want to know."

"I do."

She shook her head, her hair flying against the pillow. "Trust me—you don't."

He gave her a look and then leaned over to grab the bag, dumping it on the bed. A myriad of sex toys bounced out. "Whoa." He fingered the butt plug. "Hell, no." He tossed it over his shoulder and then shoved the restraints to the floor. Eyes gleaming, he grabbed the paddle.

She shifted against him. "You're kidding."

He swished it through the air. "Believe me, baby. I'd much rather go skin to skin with your ass." He threw the paddle aside and it fell to clatter on the floor. "When you feel a sting, it's gonna be my hand." His eyebrows arched, and he tugged the plastic package to him and ripped it open. "You ever use one of these?"

Heat filled her chest and rose to her face. "No." She'd heard of a pocket rocket, but hadn't used one. "Sorry."

Squinting, he read the plastic. "Better than anything." He bent his head and flipped a button, and a narrow cylinder started to hum. "Let's test that theory." Moving slowly, he ran the toy along her thigh.

She arched into him, her legs trembling. The ache between her legs intensified. He pressed the tip against her clit, and the vibrations dug in. She cried out.

He left it there, lightly, driving her crazy. More pressure. She needed more pressure. When he moved away, she actually whimpered.

"I can think of something better." Moving down, he sucked her clit into his mouth.

She exploded, biting her lip to keep from screaming, nails digging into her palms. He licked her, humming in pleasure. Waves bombarded her, crackled through her, forcing her to ride into a white-hot light.

Finally, she came down. Yet she somehow wanted more.

He rolled to the side of the bed, shucked his jeans, and rolled on a condom in such a smooth motion she could only gape.

"Let me free," she murmured, wanting nothing more than to flatten her hands over his ripped chest.

"No." He knelt between her legs, positioned himself, and gently slid inside her, inch after firm inch.

Pain and pleasure flared inside her, and she lifted her legs. Her thighs clasped his hips, and she breathed out. "Jesus."

He reached up and planted a hand over her wrists, holding them even tighter to the bed. Then his other arm hooked around her thigh, holding her open.

She. Couldn't. Move.

The vulnerability rippled through her on the heels of a craving that tightened her around his cock. He dropped his forehead to hers and started to thrust. She was soft and wet and primed, and she could feel him everywhere. Inside her. Around her. Controlling her.

She shouldn't like it—she knew she shouldn't like it.

She loved it. "Harder," she whispered.

He lifted up and took her mouth, driving her head back. His hips hammered him so deep inside her, she'd feel him forever. It was hard and fast and rough. She couldn't move and could only take more. More everything.

He slammed hard, and the room sheeted white. She closed her eyes, arching up into him, cascading pleasure tearing her apart. Her orgasm lasted forever, until he finally shoved home and jerked against her.

She panted against him.

Lifting his head, he pressed a soft kiss to her lips. A quick movement had her hands free. With a soft sigh of pure pleasure, she slid her palms over his shoulders, enjoying the warm play of muscle.

He grinned.

A rumble echoed.

Fire flashed and the window crashed open.

CHAPTER 18

Life takes unexpected turns. Ladies roll with them. Women up and fight. ~ The Lady Elks Secret Archives.

HAWK JUMPED UP, reaching for Dawn and carrying her through the door to the living room.

"That was an explosion." Colton was already running down the stairs, Glock in hand, his wife behind him.

Another explosion destroyed the night, and Hawk turned to grab a blanket to wrap around Dawn. Placing her behind the couch, he ducked back into the guest room and grasped his jeans, tugging them on and reaching for his gun. He stalked into the living room, where Colt already was looking out at a burning barn.

Melanie clutched her stomach, her eyes wide. "Hawk? You're cut."

"Glass from the explosion," he muttered, taking a spot next to Colton. "The force blew our window in."

Colton leaned to the side, back to a wall. "You see anything?"

"No." Hawk took several deep breaths, his instincts

humming. "This isn't like Meyer, a full on assault." He'd thought they'd be safe and had fully expected Meyer to flee like the coward he was.

Melanie held her phone out. "I'm on the line with 911. Help's on the way."

A pattering of gunfire lit across the house. Hawk jumped over the couch, taking Dawn down, landing square and covering her. He glanced to see Colton sprawled over a struggling Melanie. Without missing a beat, he tugged Dawn up, keeping low. Smoke filtered in through the holes in the walls. "Follow me."

Colton did so, and they ran through the kitchen to the cellar doors.

Hawk nudged Dawn toward the top step. "Get down and stay there until I come for you."

She was pale but steady. "I can shoot."

"I know." He ran a knuckle down the side of her face. The woman was smart and strong, and he needed her to protect Melanie, who could barely move. Yeah. Dawn could handle things. "The gun safe is down there. Arm yourself and wait for a signal." He eyed Melanie and her huge belly. "Take care of Mel."

Dawn gave him a short nod before reaching to help Melanie down the stairs. Melanie shrugged her off and reached for the wall. "I can shoot, too," she muttered, determination in her tone.

Colton shut the door, fury darkening his face.

"Fire out the front, Colton." Hawk breathed out of his nose and drew on his training, gun in hand. "I'll be back in a minute."

Colton opened his mouth to argue, glanced at the closed door to the cellar, and then nodded.

Hawk released a breath. No matter what, Colton wouldn't let anybody go past him to that door. The front door burst open, and gunfire ripped through the wall. "Down!" He pivoted and ducked, lungs heating as Colt took aim and fired, dropping one guy.

Hawk dove and rolled, taking the guy's gun and coming up firing. A second man fell, landing face first.

"Rain? You there, buddy?" a voice called out through the crackling fire.

Hawk's lids lowered, and he mouthed *Meyer* to Colton.

Colt's nostrils flared.

Hawk gestured, waited for another nod, and then inched around the sofa toward the kitchen. He waited until Colt had kicked shut the damaged door and taken position at the busted window.

Colton fired out, just for measure.

Good move. Hawk reached the back door and jumped into a pair of Colton's boots before drawing on one of Colt's jackets. Good thing they were about the same size. He headed outside, catching his breath at the freezing rain. Ducking his head, he kept against the house and angled toward the front. A guy stood guard, one of Meyer's, and Hawk cracked him on the back of the head. He went down without a sound.

An explosion ripped from the front of the house, and Hawk stopped breathing.

Grenade? The bastard had grenades? So much for being in Canada and then fleeing. This was well planned.

Forgetting all training, Hawk ran around the front just in time to see Meyer step over the demolished boards of the front porch and into the house. All Hawk could see was Colton's prone legs.

Hawk lunged into a full run behind Meyer, who'd just cleared the couch.

Dawn stood in the kitchen doorway, shotgun in hand. Her face beyond pale, her eyes wide, she pulled the trigger.

Meyer ducked to the side, and Hawk hit him in a full-on tackle, sending them both sprawling across sharp embers.

Dawn screamed. Thank heavens she hadn't just shot him.

Grunting and throwing punches, they rolled around, fires

lighting on their jackets. They were evenly matched in muscle and training, but Hawk went primal. This was his home, and Meyer had breached it.

He fought like he held the devil, finally ending up on top and hitting Meyer so hard under the jaw, his head snapped back, and he went lax. Hawk breathed heavily, his gaze searching Dawn.

She remained standing, gun in hand. "Colton," she whispered, running toward the downed man.

Colton groaned and shoved himself up, blood dripping down his head. "Ouch." He wiped off his cheekbone. "That Meyer?"

Sirens trilled outside, and several trucks lurched to a stop. Hawk nodded. Too bad the bastard was out and not dead. Yeah, Hawk would consider just cutting his throat, but not with Dawn watching, and probably not on Melanie's floor. Even though it was destroyed.

Quinn ran inside, gun out, gaze taking in the destroyed room. "Our two guards are unconscious near the north tree line —knocked out cold. What in the world?"

Hawk shoved off Meyer. "My fault. Never saw him coming right at us. Too much to risk." He'd believed Zonas in the hospital. Perhaps the guy hadn't known the truth about Meyer. Perhaps the guy had purposely misled him. It really didn't matter, considering Meyer had attacked directly, apparently figuring it was the only way. Two strides forward and Hawk gently secured the rifle from Dawn before drawing her up and into his arms. "You did good."

She slowly turned as Melanie crossed into the room, hands on her stomach. "Mel's water broke."

At the words, Melanie Freeze doubled over with a soft cry.

* * *

DAWN SAT in the backseat of the truck, Melanie's legs over hers while Hawk drove hell-bent for the hospital. Colton sat in the passenger seat, half conscious, a bag of ice to his head. Even so, he was half turned around, his fingers entangled with Melanie's. With the freezing rain and terrible storm, there had been several accidents, and though Quinn and the fire department had showed up, the ambulances were all out on calls.

There wasn't time to wait for an ambulance.

Melanie's body stiffened, and she cried out. Colton almost climbed over the seat, and Dawn shoved him back. Blood poured from his head. Hawk had looked him over and decided he'd been hit by flying debris and not shot, so that was something.

Dawn patted Melanie's arm and smoothed down the blanket covering her friend. "You're okay, Mel. We'll be there soon." But they were in a rural area, with icy roads, and by the tightening of Mel's stomach, soon wouldn't be good. They needed *now*.

"Quinn should've come with us," Melanie moaned. "He knows how to deliver a baby, right?"

Dawn bit her lip. "Probably. But the barn was still on fire and there were men to arrest. Quinn had to stay there." She gulped down air. This was Melanie's first time having a baby, or babies, and surely it took a longer time than this. "I'm sure we're fine and have plenty of time to reach the hospital. If not, I can deliver the babies. I've been reading up on it." Not. Not at all.

Melanie snorted. "You are such a terrible liar." Her body clenched, and her legs extended. "Oh. I need to push. Right now. I need to."

No. It was too soon. Dawn patted her knee. "I'm sure we have plenty of time."

Colton convulsed and went limp in the front seat.

Hawk grabbed his shoulder. "Colt?"

Dawn's brother didn't move. Her eyes met Hawk's worried ones in the rearview mirror.

Melanie arched and screamed.

"Hawk, we need to stop," Dawn whispered, her gaze caught on Melanie's morphing tummy. Maybe they'd run out of time?

"No." Mel punched the back of Hawk's seat. "Colton is out cold, and he needs a doctor now. Just go faster."

Hawk pressed on the gas, his knuckles turning white on the wheel.

"Um, Mel?" Dawn asked, her gut roiling. "Should I take a look or something?" The woman was still in her nightgown, so it wouldn't be a big deal, right? "It's not like we haven't seen each other naked before." They'd been shopping together their whole lives. "Just a peek?"

"Erg." Melanie sucked in a pained breath. "Go ahead."

Dawn took a deep breath and lifted Mel's skirt before dropping it quickly. Her stomach plunged to her feet, and probably farther. "Um. So. I can see a head. Is that bad?"

Hawk half turned. "You can see a head?"

"Yeah." Dawn bit her lip. "Definite baby head."

Hawk pulled to the side of the road and quickly dialed a number. "We're at mile marker seventeen on Burnes Road. Send an ambulance. Now." He reached over and felt Colton's neck. Then he jumped out of the truck and yanked open Melanie's door, quickly climbing inside and behind her.

Melanie struggled, tears filling her eyes. "We have to get Colton to the hospital."

"He's breathing and his heartbeat is strong." Hawk shut the door, half-lifted Mel, and sat on the seat, bracketing her from behind. "Lean back against me, Mel, girl." Then he stared at Dawn over Melanie's head. "You up for this?"

No way. Dawn nodded. "Not a problem. We've been birthing foals and calves for years."

Melanie snorted. "I'm not a barnyard animal." Then she moaned, her stomach rolling visibly. "Don't do this. Don't ever, ever, ever do this."

Dawn shook her head, eyes wide. "I won't. Never." After seeing the head, she truly, truly, truly meant the words. A part of her, the sensible part, figured she'd change her mind. Not at the moment, however. "But right now, you have to push. I'll catch the baby in the blanket, and by then, the ambulance will be here?" She looked hopefully at Hawk, who grimaced. Lines had cut into the sides of his mouth, and blood from the fight still littered his neck.

But his gaze stayed strong and sure.

"We can do this," he said, tightening his hold on Melanie. "We've been together our whole lives, and we can handle this." He'd left the truck running, the heat pouring out of the vents. "All the time in the world. Let's get moving, Mel. If the head's there, I think the baby needs to come out."

Melanie stiffened, the veins in her neck standing out. She screamed, and the sound echoed through the truck. Then she grunted and pushed.

Colton jerked and turned. "What is happening?"

Melanie reached out and grabbed his hand. "Baby. Now."

Colton shifted and half came over the seat, holding her hand. "Okay. You can do this."

Dawn got ready. Melanie pushed again. And again. And then again. Sirens sounded in the distance. Finally, a shoulder emerged. Dawn tensed, her blanket ready. One more hard push, and the baby slid out.

Dawn caught a slimy bundle of goo that was already squirming. She wiped off her...niece. "It's a girl." Dawn grinned, her eyes filling, her chest rioting. She handed the bundle to Melanie, who smiled and held her tight.

Hawk's gaze met Dawn's, and so much emotion burned there she couldn't breathe. Ever again.

Then Melanie stiffened. "Oh, no." She bit her lip. "I have to push."

"Baby number two," Dawn said soothingly. It had to be just

REBECCA ZANETTI

like a cow, right? She ducked to look and then gasped. "Here it comes."

Colton stared at her. "You're doing great. All of you."

Dawn took a deep breath. "Get ready."

Suddenly, blue and red lights came around the bed, swirling through the snow.

CHAPTER 19

Family is everything. ~ The Lady Elks Secret Archives.

HAWK FINISHED SMOOTHING the very ruffled feathers of the nurse on duty, explaining that Colton had been conked in the head and then forced to watch his wife give birth on the side of a road in a storm. To twins. So his ignoring orders, basically telling the doctor to bug off, and going away from treatment and into his wife's room was perfectly reasonable.

The nurse, a battle-ax at least a thousand years old, didn't quite agree. Finally, something else caught her attention, and she turned her back on him.

Folks were beginning to pour in the front doors, no doubt to see Melanie's babies. A woman with spiked pink hair stormed up, green eyes blazing. He couldn't remember her name. "Where's Dawn?"

He smiled down at the guitar player. "You don't like me."

She pressed sharp nails on her slim hips. "You're in my way and you're holding Dawn back. She should go on tour with us."

He liked that. He could get that. "Dawn's giving her statement to the sheriff in the cafeteria down the hall."

Without another word, but adding a hard glare, the woman headed toward the cafeteria. Hawk lost his smile. Keeping an eye on the battle-ax, he sidled around the reception desk and hurried down the hallway to Melanie's room.

She lay in a bed, sound asleep, twin little cradles next to her. Colton sat by her side, an ugly purple bruise spreading across his temple and down his face. He grinned. "Thanks," he whispered.

Hawk leaned over to look at two very tiny girls. "They look like their mama." Curly brown hair, petite features, stubborn chins.

Colton nodded happily. "I know."

"How's your head?" Hawk whispered.

"Fine. I'm a little concussed." Colton noted the gun now strapped to Hawk's hip. "You're not staying."

Hawk swallowed. "No. We're hitting the storage house tonight."

Colt's gaze sizzled. "And then?"

Hawk stepped back, body going cold. "Then I'm going after the rest of the organization." His buddy had to get it. "If I don't, they'll come after me. And it's my job."

"It was your job." Colton stood and got into his face. "You're out, and it's time to move on. Meyer had a hard-on for you, but that was personal. Let somebody else take down the rest of them. You're home."

Hawk sighed. "I thought you'd get it."

"I do." Colton clapped him on the shoulder. "You promised your buddy you'd bring Meyer to justice, and you have. You did it. You're not responsible for the world, Hawk. You've done your time, and there's plenty to do here. Time to stop running."

"I'm not running." Hawk's lungs heated.

"Yeah, you are. You've always thought you needed a purpose,

needed to do something good, since you were left all alone. There's plenty of good you can do here, without getting shot at. Much." Slowly, Colton sat back down, his gaze serious. "If you leave her this time, you're gonna lose her. I know my sister."

Hawk stiffened. "You have to want her with somebody better."

"There is no one better." Colt leaned back, no give on his hard face. "I'm not going to convince you, and I'm not going to get angry with you. Either you know that in your gut, or you don't."

Hawk lifted his head. "You don't think she'll wait." He said it as a statement, not a question.

"She's waited long enough." Colton lifted a shoulder. "I'll miss you."

"Ditto." His gut clenching, his chest aching, Hawk turned and took one more look at a peacefully sleeping Melanie. "Take care of our Mel."

"Always," Colton said, standing again. He gave Hawk a hard hug and then let him go.

Hawk left the room, his mind spinning. He had to do his job, didn't he? There'd always be danger, but Colton had been right about it being personal between him and Meyer.

Dawn waited for him, arms crossed, back to the opposite wall. "You're leaving."

"Yes," he said.

"How long?" she asked.

"I don't know." He could give her the truth. "As long as it takes."

"Doesn't have to be you." Her eyes blazed, and her stubborn jaw had set.

Reese came around the corner, in full-on black flack and bulletproof gear, bruises still mottling his face.

Hawk frowned. "What do you think you're doing?"

Reese shrugged. "I'm not missing this."

"You've been discharged?" Hawk asked.

"No." Reese headed for the outside door. "We leave in five, Rain."

Hawk nodded.

Dawn shook her head. "You have to be finished proving yourself. Stay home, work the ranch, help Colton with the businesses." Never one to pull her punches, she continued, "And date me."

Which would put her in even more danger until he finished the job. "You don't understand."

"I do. But I'm done waiting for you." She glanced down the hallway. "I might not even be here when you get back. If you get back."

Hawk frowned. "You're not seriously thinking of touring with that crazy group, are you?"

"What do you care?" she asked, chin lifting.

He stepped into her, his gut hurting. "I care, Dawnie. You know I do." Her scent almost dropped him to his knees. All woman, all huckleberry.

She reached up and threaded her fingers through his hair, tugging down. Then her mouth pressed against his.

He delved deep, yanking her into him, so much softness he could drown. Holding tight, he put every ounce of feeling he owned into the kiss, slowly gentling his touch. When he lifted up, her mouth was parted, her cheeks rosy, and her eyes dreamy. Her hands caressed down his chest.

She gently pushed him back, and he went.

Facing him head on, she gave a short nod. "Bye, Hawk." Turning on a cowboy boot, she crossed the hallway and entered her sister-in-law's hospital room.

Without looking back.

CHAPTER 20

Love matters—fight for it. ~ The Lady Elks Secret Archives.

Two weeks later

Hawk carried Reese inside the hospital and dumped him in a wheelchair. He'd only been gone two weeks, and it seemed like a lifetime.

Reese groaned and punched his leg.

"Shut up." Hawk wheeled him toward a doctor. "Doc? We have a bullet wound, a couple of knife wounds, and probably a concussion here."

The doctor on duty ran forward and took the chair.

Hawk scrubbed both hands down the scruff on his face and looked for a bathroom. He had blood on his hands, a lot of it, and he needed to wash. Now it was on his face and maybe in his hair.

Then he waited…and waited…and waited, wearing his black

cargo pants, flack boots, and the bulletproof vest that now held a couple of holes.

Finally, an orderly came out and said he could go on in. He stomped into Reese's room, the same one as before, and dropped into a chair. "You're not dead."

Reese grinned, his eyes unfocused. Good pain meds, probably. "Nope. Bullet went through—just needed stitches. That was a good raid."

Yeah, it had been a good raid. "We have locations of three more drug storage places, and we have the beginning of a list of other distributors and dealers." The news, the facts, didn't even remotely excite Hawk like they would've last year. "I've handed it all over to the DEA, which kind of placated them about our going in alone. So you can just get better," Hawk said.

Reese grimaced and settled back on the pillows. "I'll be back in action soon."

Hawk frowned. "No you won't. Geez. You've been in the hospital constantly. Aren't you tired of it? Tired of getting shot and stabbed?"

"Yeah, but they're still out there," Reese said.

"Sure, and they'll always be out there." Hawk rolled his shoulders and let the sense of home finally fill the emptiness inside his chest. "We did it. We brought Meyer to justice, and we closed down his operations. There will always be more. I'm tired of hunting people down for mistakes in their past, so I should probably start actually living in the present. Let's let somebody else get them—let the DEA, who you no longer work for, do their jobs. Take some of the cushy security jobs and get off the front lines. What do you think?"

Reese studied him. "You're done?"

Hawk bit his lip. He'd wanted to come home for so long, and then he'd had a home, and he'd messed it up. "Yeah." His breath eased out as if he'd been holding it for years. "I'm done."

"Well, Dawn Freeze is definitely worth it." Reese grinned.

Hawk shook his head. "I screwed up," he muttered.

Reese nodded. "I know Dawn, and she's a sweetheart. She'll forgive you."

Sweet? Yeah, Dawn Freeze was sweet. She was also mean as could be if necessary, and he'd earned mean.

The doctor strode in. "I need a minute or two to check those stitches," he said with a pointed look at Hawk.

Hawk rolled his eyes and stretched to his feet, heading out to the waiting room. Mrs. Hudson and Mrs. Poppins perched like birds on branches in the bright orange chairs.

His body stiffened, and he forced a smile. He approached and took a seat. "Ladies?"

Mrs. Hudson cleared her throat and sat forward. "Sharon at the front desk told us you were here."

He sighed. "Ah. I appreciate your attempts to matchmake—"

"Oh, no." Mrs. Poppins shook her head, sending spiral gray curls winging. "We're not. Well, not with you. You have to go, Hawk. You'll mess everything up again."

He blinked. "Excuse me?"

Mrs. Hudson drew a nicely stitched pillow from her over-sized bag. "Dawn gave it back, because she failed. So sad. Then we figured, Dawn hadn't failed. You did. We just needed to get a different stallion in the gate for her, you know?"

Hawk frowned and took the pillow. *How to Catch a Man.* "Huh?"

"We picked the wrong man." Mrs. Hudson twittered, clapping her hands together. "Now that Dawn is going to travel with the band for a year, and now that Adam is going, too, she has another chance with the rules. It's so simple."

Hawk's head lifted slowly, his brain roaring into gear. Fast. "Excuse me?"

Mrs. Poppins leaned toward him. "Yes. See, she can start all over with Adam and follow the rules. They'll be engaged before they get home from tour. The boy plays a mean guitar, you know." She smiled, all wrinkly happiness, at Mrs. Hudson. "It all worked out perfectly, Patty. You're so smart."

"I'm a born matchmaker," Mrs. Hudson said, faded eyes filled with pleasure. "We talked to Adam, and he agreed that since you're out of the way, he feels okay making a play for Dawn now."

Mrs. Poppins pushed her thick glasses back up her nose. "Yes. We had no idea. He moved aside because of his friendship with you, Hawk, and now that you and Dawn are over for good, he finally stepped up." She shook her head. "I don't know how we didn't see it before. They're perfect for each other. Just perfect."

"Yes." Mrs. Hudson adjusted her bedazzled jeans, contentment in her sigh. "They both are into business, and they both love music. Why we didn't see it in the first place, I'll never know." Her pointed chin lowered, and she focused on Hawk. "While we love you, sweetie, you really must leave town until the day after tomorrow. After Dawn and Adam go on tour, then you can come back. We could even help you find a nice girl."

Mrs. Poppins nodded. "Yes. How about Anne Newberry? She could really use a man."

Hawk held up a hand. "No. What do you mean, Dawn's leaving?"

"Oh. Well, they have what I guess is called a 'gig' in Berlin the day after tomorrow, so they're flying out tomorrow. The goodbye party for Sizzled Pink is over at the Elks Lodge right now." Mrs. Hudson gasped and pushed to her bony feet. "We should really get back, Bernie. They'll be looking for us."

"Oh. You're so right." Mrs. Poppins stood. "Ah, may we have the pillow back?"

Hawk's entire world narrowed to the moment. His past, his present, and then his future flashed in front of his eyes so quickly, he swayed. His head snapped up. "No." Holding tight to the soft fabric, he ignored Mrs. Hudson's shocked "oh my" and turned to stalk out of the hospital and into the billowing snow.

Dawn and Adam on some European adventure? Oh, hell no.

* * *

DAWN GLANCED around at all the decorations sprawling from one end of the Elk's bar to the other. "It looks like a zombie barfed pink all over."

Luann snorted and batted at a pink balloon. "I know, right? And I usually love pink."

Dawn laughed and noted the heart-shaped cookies over on a table. "Even the cookies are different shades." So sweet and cute. Women milled around, eating and chatting, but the scents of bourbon and pipe tobacco still hung in the air with a sense of welcome.

Luann glanced around, her purple hair fitting right in. "I guess I see it. I mean, why you'd want to stay here."

Dawn smiled. "I know. So many people search the world for this. For the sense of family and home."

The outside door opened, and she felt it. The swell of angry, branding, vibrating heat.

She rose to her feet as a defense, her entire body going on full alert. Her heart beat harder, and a fiery relief rippled through her. He was safe. How she'd missed him.

Hawk stood planted in the entryway, in full combat gear— badass boots, dark pants, bulletproof vest, finished off with fresh bruises across his cheekbone.

"Oh my," Luann breathed next to her. "Just...oh my."

His green gaze landed hard on Dawn, pinning her in place. "No," he said.

She belatedly noted both the pillow and the coiled rope in his hand. "Uh—" From the corner of her eye, she could see her mom and sisters-in-law drawing near, beaming smiles.

"You are not going to Europe with Sizzled Pink," Hawk said evenly, kicking a rolling pink balloon out of his way.

She caught her breath. "Uh—"

"I screwed up, and I get that." He waved the pillow around. "But apparently so did you."

Her mouth dropped open, and she sucked in air.

"But *I* met the rules, and I get to win." He glanced down and read number one. "'Make your man the only man around.'" He glanced up, a muscle working in his jaw. "I've made you the only woman in the world for me since the day you turned eighteen. There is nobody else, and there will never be anybody else."

Around her, Dawn could hear sighs. Long, drawn out, dreamy sighs.

"Um—" she whispered.

"I'm not done." He glanced down at the pillow. "'Don't give the cow away.'" His lips tipped. "Well, I did hold out for years, waiting. I mean, you started throwing yourself at me in your teens, skinny-dipping in the pond, and I always was the gentleman, even though you made it very difficult."

Dawn bit her lip. Her mother harrumphed and shook her head.

Hawk nodded. "Yep. I'd say I passed that one. Number three? 'The way to a man's heart...'" He tapped the pillow against his side. "Well, now, Dawnie. I didn't have time to make you dinner tonight, but you stay with me and I'll cook any time you want. I promise, not once will I send you to the hospital."

A twittering of female laughter ran through the crowd.

Hawk read number four. "'Let your man rescue you.'" He looked up, lids going heavy, gaze softening. "You saved my ass that night we went off the side of the road, and you know it. Besides that, the very thought of you, the idea that someday, maybe, you'd be mine, kept me alive in wars a world away."

The feminine sighing upped in volume around the room.

Dawn's knees wobbled. "Hawk—"

He tossed the pillow to the side, and Loni Freeze caught it, holding it close to her stomach. He sobered, lifted the rope, and twirled. Almost in slow motion, it soared through the air, and landed squarely over Dawn's head, dropping around her. Well experienced, he tugged at just the right moment, binding her arms to her sides. Hand-over-hand, he coiled the rope until his warmth brushed her front. "You've been chasing me for years, baby, and it's time I caught you."

Tears filled her eyes.

He reached out and lifted her chin with one knuckle. "It's always been you, Dawn Freeze. I love you. Give me another chance—I'm here for good. I promise."

She sniffled and then smiled. Everything she wanted stood in front of her, giving her the world. Giving her...him. It was more than she'd ever dreamed. "You know it's always been you. I love you, Hawk."

The room erupted with cheers, but she didn't really notice, because Hawk's mouth covered hers. With promise and heat, he dove deep, taking her heart with him.

Finally, he straightened up. "I love you." Then he glanced around at all the pink. "Sorry about the European trip and ruining your going away party."

Dawn frowned, her mind clicking into gear. "I told Luann the other day that I wasn't going."

Mrs. Hudson and Mrs. Poppins giggled near the side doorway.

Dawn glanced from them and then back up at Hawk. "Um, this is Melanie's baby shower, Hawk."

He stilled. His eyes went liquid. Then he threw back his head and laughed, the sound filling her heart with the future. "It's great to be home."

Dawn leaned into him, pushing out of the rope. "For good this time."

He smiled and kissed her again. "Yeah. You and me. Forever."

* * *

CATCH UP with the Montana Maverick's with Adam's story in Holding the Reins!

She came to town for a movie. She never expected a real-life romantic thriller…

Bianca Estrada is in Montana for one reason—secure the perfect location for a Hollywood blockbuster and move on. The job means everything. It's her chance to pay off debts that were never hers to begin with. But someone in town doesn't want the film to happen, and the escalating threats make it clear they'll do whatever it takes to scare her off.

Adam Ridgeway has built a quiet life as the owner of the local bar, far removed from his Army days and the heartbreak he swore never to repeat. The last thing he needs is to play hero for a city girl with one foot out the door. But when danger follows Bianca straight into his world, keeping his distance is no longer an option.

The only thing more persistent than Bianca's stalker? The town's meddling matchmakers, determined to push her and Adam together at every turn. With danger closing in and chemistry burning hot, what starts as protection turns into something deeper. But with Bianca's future miles away and Adam's roots planted firmly in Montana, can they hold on to each other when the credits roll?

* * *

OR, are you in the mood for a small town romance with more than a hint of mystery? Check out what's happening in the Albertini world with Tessa's romance in Tessa's Trust. Here's a quick excerpt:

Apparently, there wasn't any sort of seating order at McCloskey's. I'd seen speed dating on television and thought the moving party had to shift to the next table. Apparently not. I scrutinized Nick. "Well?"

"Well, what?" he muttered.

"You're supposed to charm me."

He cocked his head, looking way too handsome under the soft lights above the tables. "I'm supposed to charm you?"

"Yeah. You think you can?"

"A challenge? Oh, baby, if I wanted to charm you, your socks would be off," he retorted instantly.

I chuckled. That was one thing about Nick. He was quick with a comeback. He was probably amazing in court.

"What are you doing on this side of the pass anyway?" I asked.

"It's the day after Christmas," he said. "I went snowmobiling with my brothers and returned to the family home just in time to catch my grandmother's call. You know, about her flat tire."

"Oh, that. I've heard there's a flat tire bandit going around town," I murmured. "They must have gotten Gerty."

Nick just watched me, reminding me of a hawk about to dive hard on scurrying prey. "Are you still mad at me?"

I swallowed. While I understood he'd only been doing his job, the guy had issued my arrest warrant, probably instinctively knowing I didn't do it. "Yes."

"Can't blame you." Man, his voice was smooth. Like good whiskey poured over ice. "But I had a job to do, and I knew your lawyer would take care of you. I couldn't appear to give you favoritism."

I didn't want to be fair about that, but I did understand. "Fair enough."

He sighed. "Why are you in Silverville tonight?"

I lost my smile and reached for my Prosecco again. I was proud of what I'd accomplished, but even so, my voice softened just a little when I spoke. "I bought Silver Sadie's." Then I looked down at my glass.

He was quiet for a moment. "Wow."

I looked up. "Would you care to expound on that statement?"

"That's impressive," he said. "People have been trying to get Sadie to sell for years."

"It took me months," I admitted. "We've been negotiating for quite a while." I gestured down the line of tables toward Bobbo. "Hence date number one."

Nick's grin reached his eyes. "You have to go on more dates with Bobbo?"

"Oh, no. Just one with Bobbo, but then his other two brothers, as well."

The look of amusement slid out of Nick's eyes. "You're not going on a date with Eddie."

Eddie was the middle great-nephew, and I didn't know much about him.

"I am. It's in the contract," I said.

Nick leaned forward, a muscle ticking in his jaw. "Your sister let you sign a contract that forces you to go on a date with Eddie Brando?"

I reared up, and even my ears heated. "My sister didn't *let* me do anything. I read the contract. I understood it. I was happy with it, and I signed it."

Nick's chin lowered. "You are not going on a date with Eddie Brando."

"Listen, Nick," I said, "I'm sure you're used to being all bossy with everybody in your office, but I'm not in your world. I don't work for you, and you're not going to tell me what to do."

Pretty much nothing in the world could have stopped me from going on a date with Eddie Brando at that point.

"You're as unreasonable as your sister," he muttered.

"Don't you talk about my sister like that." Heat raced through my veins.

True, Anna had made some miscalculations when working for Nick that had ended with her getting fired, but she was happier than happy could be owning her own law firm. "She was the best lawyer you've ever had in your office."

"Yeah, she was," he said quietly. "And she let her personal life cloud her judgment."

Was that a direct hit? It felt like it. My foot tensed.

"You kick me, and we're going to have a problem." His gaze turned piercing.

I stilled. When Basanelli issued a threat, it came across clean. I had to respect that. Also, I had barely moved my foot. How did he know I wanted to kick him? "My guess is most women want to kick you," I retorted.

"It's possible, but I strongly recommend you don't." Then he just waited, watching me patiently. It was almost a dare.

Maybe that was how I earned the *wild* moniker. I could never refuse a dare. So, I kicked him. It was just with my snow boot, which wasn't even a little pointy and glanced off his shin. Even so, it pushed his chair back a little bit.

Then I waited. Oh, the bubbly had most certainly gone to my head.

One of his dark eyebrows rose, and then his lids lowered to half-mast. He was fully Italian, and I'd expected something... more. Was I disappointed? Maybe. I didn't want Nick to be a guy I could push around. Not that it mattered what kind of guy he was, but still.

"You're all talk," I said.

"What makes you say that?" His voice was velvet over steel, and an unwilling tremble ticked down my spine.

"I kicked you," I said unnecessarily.

His chin lifted just enough to give him a predatory look. "I'm well aware you just made the colossal mistake of kicking me in the middle of McCloskey's. I meant every word I said. You will regret it." He crossed his arms, flexing pretty impressive chest muscles, and his smile sent butterflies winging through my stomach...mainly because it wasn't a smile. What was that look?

"You didn't think I'd make you regret it right here, right now, did you?"

I kind of had. I figured he'd snap at me or stomp away. "Yes." I forced a smile.

"Oh, no, baby," he said so softly I leaned forward to hear him better. "I'm the most patient man you'll ever meet. I have no problem biding my time."

I lost the smile.

Check out Tessa's story in Tessa's Trust!

ACKNOWLEDGMENTS

Thank you to everyone who helped bring this story of love, laughter, and a town that just won't mind its own business to life. If I forgot anyone, blame the matchmaking Lady Elks or the town gossip chain—it's hard to keep track when everyone is scheming to set up the hero and heroine.

To Big Tone, my rock through every storm, whether it is brainstorming over coffee or patiently enduring my cowboy jokes, which, let's be honest, are utterly fantastic. Your support reminds me that every dream needs a steady foundation.

To Gabe, who proves that chaos can be handled with humor, grace, and a bit of stubbornness. Whether it is runaway deadlines or runaway cattle, you keep things grounded.

To Karlina, whose creativity adds the perfect touch of magic. Without you, this story might have been all spreadsheets and cow wrangling—thank you for bringing the sparkle.

To Kathleen Sweeney and the Book Brush team, for crafting a cover that captures not just the rugged beauty of Montana, but also the heart of a best-friend's-little-sister romance.

To Caitlin Blasdell, my literary compass, for keeping me from veering completely off the publishing trail. Your wisdom makes every story sharper, funnier, and full of heart.

To Stella Bloom, for bringing these characters to life with warmth and wit. Your voice adds the charm of a small-town potluck without the questionable casseroles.

To Anissa Beatty, Gabi Brockelsby, Leanna Feazel, Madison

Fairbanks, and Rebecca's Rebels for your enthusiasm, support, and keen eyes. You are as reliable as a Montana sunrise.

To Writerspace, for helping connect readers with their next great romance. Your matchmaking skills extend beyond books.

To my family and friends, thank you for cheering me on even when I talk about fictional cowboys more than real-life updates.

And finally, to you, dear reader, for diving into this story of love, laughter, and a town that refuses to stay out of it. I hope it sweeps you into Montana, makes you chuckle at the meddling, and warms your heart with a romance that was meant to be. Thank you for coming along for the ride. You are the reason I keep writing stories filled with laughter, love, and just a touch of chaos.

READING ORDER

I know a lot of you like the exact reading order for each series, so here you go as of the release of this book, although if you read most novels out of order, it's okay.

KNIFE'S EDGE, ALASKA SERIES

1. Dead of Winter
2. Thaw of Spring

THE ANNA ALBERTINI FILES

1. Disorderly Conduct
2. Bailed Out
3. Adverse Possession
4. Holiday Rescue novella
5. Santa's Subpoena
6. Holiday Rogue novella
7. Tessa's Trust
8. Holiday Rebel novella

9. Habeas Corpus
10. Celtic Justice

LAUREL SNOW SERIES

1. You Can Run
2. You Can Hide
3. You Can Die
4. You Can Kill

GRIMM BARGAINS SERIES

1. One Cursed Rose
2. One Dark Kiss

DEEP OPS SERIES

1. Hidden
2. Taken novella
3. Fallen
4. Shaken novella (in Pivot Anthology)
5. Broken
6. Driven
7. Unforgiven
8. Frostbitten

MONTANA MAVERICK SERIES

1. Against the Wall
2. Under the Covers
3. Rising Assets
4. Over the Top
5. Holding the Reins

Dark Protectors/Enforcers/1001 DN

1. Fated (Dark Protectors Book 1)
2. Claimed (Dark Protectors Book 2)
3. Tempted novella (Dark Protectors 2.5)
4. Hunted (Dark Protectors Book 3)
5. Consumed (Dark Protectors Book 4)
6. Provoked (Dark Protectors Book 5)
7. Twisted Novella (Dark Protectors 5.5)
8. Shadowed (Dark Protectors Book 6)
9. Tamed Novella (Dark Protectors 6.5)
10. Marked (Dark Protectors Book 7)
11. Wicked Ride (Realm Enforcers 1)
12. Wicked Edge (Realm Enforcers 2)
13. Wicked Burn (Realm Enforcers 3)
14. Talen Novella (Dark Protectors 7.5)
15. Wicked Kiss (Realm Enforcers 4)
16. Wicked Bite (Realm Enforcers 5)
17. Teased (Reese Bros. novella)
18. Tricked (Reese Bros. novella)
19. Tangled (Reese Bros. novella)
20. Vampire's Faith (Dark Protectors 8) ***A great entry point for series***
21. Demon's Mercy (Dark Protectors 9)
22. Vengeance (Rebels novella)
23. Alpha's Promise (Dark Protectors 10)
24. Hero's Haven (Dark Protectors 11)
25. Vixen (Rebels novella)
26. Guardian's Grace (Dark Protectors 12)
27. Vampire (Rebels novella)
28. Rebel's Karma (Dark Protectors 13)
29. Immortal's Honor (Dark Protector 14)
30. A Vampire's Kiss (Rebels novella)

31. Garrett's Destiny (Dark Protectors 15)
32. Warrior's Hope (Dark Protectors 16)
33. A Vampire's Mate (Rebels novella)
34. Prince of Darkness (DP 17)

STOPE PACKS (wolf shifters)

1. Wolf
2. Alpha
3. Shifter
4. Predator

SIN BROTHERS/BLOOD BROTHERS

1. Forgotten Sins
2. Sweet Revenge
3. Blind Faith
4. Total Surrender
5. Deadly Silence
6. Lethal Lies
7. Twisted Truths

SCORPIUS SYNDROME SERIES

Scorpius Syndrome/The Brigade Novellas

1. Scorpius Rising
2. Blaze Erupting
3. Power Surging - TBA
4. Chaos Consuming - TBA

Scorpius Syndrome Novels

1. Mercury Striking

WHAT TO READ NEXT

I often get asked what book or series of mine people should read first. All books are in written in past tense except for the Grimm Bargains books, which are in present tense. All of my books, regardless of genre, have suspense and humor in them— as well as romance, of course.

ROMANTIC SUSPENSE SERIES:

Deep Ops:

This series is about a ragtag group of misfits at Homeland Defense that create a team with each member finding love during a suspenseful time. Each book features the romance of a different couple, told through multiple POVs. Their mascots are a German Shepherd who likes to wear high heels because he feels short, and a cat named Cat that likes to live in pockets and eat goldfish. The crackers, not real fish. Probably. The series starts with Hidden and continues on with new books being released every year. There are two novellas included with anthologies as well.

Sin and Blood Brothers:

These seven books are about brothers created in a lab years ago who've gotten free while still being hunted by the scientists and the military man who trained them. They each find love and romance during a suspenseful time. Each book features the romance of a different couple, told through multiple POVs. The first four books are called the Sin Brothers and then the next three are a spinoff called the Blood Brothers. The series starts with Forgotten Sins.

The Scorpius Syndrome:

This is a post-apocalyptic romance series. A bacteria wiped out 99% of the human race. For survivors, it affects their brains, either making them more intelligent, sociopathic, or animalistic. Jax Mercury, ex-gang member and ex-serviceman, returns to LA to create an inner city sanctuary against all of the danger out there, while hopefully finding a cure. Each book is a suspenseful romance between two people told in multiple POVs. The first book is Mercury Striking. There are four prequel novellas called The Brigade, and the first one is called Scorpius Rising.

Knife's Edge, Alaska

These feature four brothers who've returned to their small Alaskan town in the middle of nowhere. Each book features the romance of one of the brothers along with a suspenseful situation that's solved by the end. The books are told in multiple POVs. The first book is Dead of Winter.

Montana Mavericks:

These books are set in Montana in a small town with a bit of suspense in each one. The romance is the focus of these, and there's some good humor. This is a band of brothers type of romance with a very involved and rather funny family. They'd be considered category romances and have dual POVs. The first book is Against the Wall.

Anna Albertini Files:

I wasn't sure where to categorize these stories. They lean more toward women's fiction or even chick lit, featuring small-town hijinks as Anna solves a new case in each story. She has a very meddling family and ends up in very humorous situations while solving cases as a lawyer. In the first book, it appears she has three potential love interests (but only ends up with one), and by the second book, the love interest is obvious and develops each book. Fans love him. This is told in Anna's POV in first person, past tense. The first book is Disorderly Conduct.

There are Christmas novellas as well, each featuring one of the Albertini brothers' romance, and these are told in multiple POVs and third person. The first Christmas novella is called Holiday Rescue.

Redemption, Wyoming Series:

This one features a group of men from around the world who were kidnapped and forced to work as mercenaries for years. They escaped and have made their way to Wyoming, trying to live normal lives as ranchers with a clubhouse. Their motto is: If it can be ridden, we ride it. (Meaning horses, snow-mobiles, motorcycles...LOL). So far, the three prequel novellas have been published, and they're each in an anthology. I should have a date for the series launching soon.

ROMANTIC THRILLER SERIES:

The Laurel Snow Thrillers

These feature Laurel Snow, who's an awkward genius and profiler now working out of her smallish Washington State home with a team - many readers love the secondary characters as well. There's a slow burn romance with Fish and Wildlife Officer Huck Rivers, and each book involves a case. There are different POVs in this one, and a really fun antagonist who readers love to hate. The first book is called You Can Run.

PARANORMAL ROMANCE SERIES:

The Dark Protectors

This series launched my career and is still going strong. The main characters are brothers who are vampires at war with other species. The vampires, demons, shifters, witches, and Fae are all just different species. They can go into sunlight, eat steak, and quite enjoy immortality. They only take blood in fighting or sex. There are fated mates, and once they mate, it's forever with a bite, brand, and sex. They can't turn anybody into a different species.The first book is called Fated. There's a spinoff that's really part of the main series, and the first book is called Wicked Ride. Then there's a great entry point for the series (a new arc) called Vampire's Faith. Each book in these features a new couple and is told in multiple POVs.

Stope Pack Wolf Shifters

This is a paranormal series featuring wolf shifters set in Washington state. It's sexy and fun. The first two books feature the same couple, and the rest of the books feature a new couple's romance. These are told in dual POVs, and the first book is called Wolf. Yeah, it's kind of on point. LOL.

DARK ROMANCE SERIES:

Grimm Bargains

This is a dark romance series featuring retellings of fairy-tales set in the modern world. Through time, four main families have learned to exchange health and vitality with certain crystals, and in today's day and age, they use these crystals to power social media companies. They have mafia ties. This series is in first person, present tense - told from various POVs. It's my only present tense series. It is dark (not hugely dark compared to some of the dark romances out there), so check the trigger warnings. The first book is called One Cursed Rose, and it's a dark retelling of Beauty and the Beast.

ABOUT THE AUTHOR

New York Times, USA Today, Publisher's Weekly, Wall Street Journal and Amazon #1 bestselling author Rebecca Zanetti has published more than eighty novels and novellas, which have been translated into several languages, with millions of copies sold worldwide. Her books have received Publisher's Weekly, Library Journal, and Kirkus starred reviews, favorable Washington Post and New York Times Book Reviews, and have been included in Amazon best books of the year.

Rebecca has ridden in a locked Chevy trunk, has asked the unfortunate delivery guy to release her from a set of handcuffs, and has discovered the best silver mine shafts in which to bury a body...all in the name of research. Honest. Find Rebecca at: www.RebeccaZanetti.com

Made in the USA
Monee, IL
07 May 2025

17065703R00122